WALT DISNEY'S

and the

MYSTERY AT MOONSTONE BAY

Authorized Edition featuring ANNETTE,
star of motion pictures and television

By DORIS SCHROEDER

Illustrations by
ADAM SZWEJKOWSKI

Cover art by Al Andersen

DISNEP
PRESS

NEW YORK

Printed in the United States of America

First Edition
1 3 5 7 9 10 8 6 4 2

Library of Congress Catalog Card Number on file.

ISBN 0-7868-4560-0
For more Disney Press fun, visit www.disneybooks.com

Contents

1   *An Old Friend*

Annette stood in the bright June sunshine and waved to her best friend, Lisa Kerry, as the train to Arizona pulled out of the station.

Lisa's lips formed the words "Come as soon as you can!" as she was carried out of Annette's sight, and Annette nodded and smiled.

But Annette wasn't smiling so happily when the train had disappeared beyond the railroad yard, and she had climbed into her neat little white sports car, nicknamed the Monster, to drive home. She had planned to be on that train with Lisa, and now she wasn't sure just when she and her Aunt Lila would be able to accept Lisa's mother's invitation to come to Pine Mesa for a summer visit.

The two girls had enjoyed an exciting time at Lisa's desert home during the Easter holidays, and had planned ever since to start the long summer vacation with a few weeks there. However, they had needed to change their plans and postpone Annette's trip until later. So now Lisa was on her way home alone.

Annette stopped at the Choc Shop, near the big high school, with a vague hope that maybe some of her crowd would be there and she would feel a little more cheerful after a bit of a gabfest.

But of all her friends, only Jinks Bradley, her next-door neighbor on the quiet side street where she lived, was to be seen. And he, wrapped in gloom, was dreaming over a double-decker sundae down at the end of the counter.

"Hi!" Jinks looked surprised to see her. "I thought you and Lisa had started for Pine Mesa! Did she change her mind? Do you think she'd like to go dancing tonight?" Jinks was digging into his pocket for a dime for the phone call even while he was asking her the question.

"Hold it!" Annette grinned and shook her head. "She's on her way. I just saw her off. No dancing tonight, Romeo."

"Aw, gosh!" Jinks was downcast. He went

back for another spoonful of ice cream. "How come you and your Aunt Lila didn't go, after all?"

"Uncle Archie had to go East on business, and Aunt Lila decided it was better to wait till he came back. She didn't want to leave the house unoccupied, and besides, she promised to take good care of his prize rose garden till he came home," Annette replied.

"Why didn't you go without her?" Jinks asked curiously. "Wouldn't she let you?"

"She wanted me to," Annette explained quickly, "but I knew that if I did, she'd be sure to get all involved entertaining Uncle Archie's business friends at the beach house and never get away. And I know how much she wants to meet Lisa's folks and see their inn on the desert." She laughed. "So I'm hanging around to snatch her away the minute Uncle Archie arrives, before he can think up any reasons to ask her to stay home!"

Annette was very fond of both her Aunt Lila and her bachelor uncle, Archie McCleod. They were her father's sister and brother, and had been like second parents to her since the accident, several years ago, that had taken both her mother's and father's lives.

Annette was telling the truth. Aunt Lila had urged her to go ahead to Arizona on the train with Lisa, but Annette had stuck to her guns. "You'll love the Kerrys and their desert-style inn. And I intend to see that you don't give up a chance to have a nice vacation *this* year," she had told Aunt Lila firmly.

And Aunt Lila, happy because of Annette's thoughtfulness, had promised to be ready to leave with her for Arizona the very second Uncle Archie was safely home among his rosebushes again.

Jinks was gloomy because he couldn't go. He had had an exciting time when he was there with the girls during Easter vacation, but he was all signed up for the summer as a lifeguard at State Beach.

He was ordering his third sundae when Annette dashed on home. She felt sorry for Jinks right now, knowing how lonely he was, but she also felt sure he would get over his gloom the moment a few pretty bathing girls smiled at him admiringly on the beach the next day.

Aunt Lila was out in the front yard, patiently digging around Uncle Archie's pet roses, as Annette drove up and turned into the driveway.

"Hi!" Annette called. "Any news?"

Aunt Lila shook her head, smiling, and Annette drove into the garage out of the bright sunlight.

When she came out a moment later, the phone was ringing inside the house. I hope that's Uncle Archie, Annette told herself. She made a dash for the back door to get to the phone before it stopped ringing.

But before she could reach the living room, the ringing stopped, and she heard Aunt Lila's voice, a little out of breath. She had evidently done some running herself.

"Oh, hello, Archie," she was saying. "How are you?"

Annette smiled happily and crossed her fingers

for luck. Oh, boy! Hope he's coming home right away! Arizona, here we come! Annette thought.

She hurried in to get the news. Aunt Lila was listening and nodding. Evidently, Uncle Archie had a lot of things to tell her. Annette could hardly wait.

Then, finally, "Of course, Archie. We'd be delighted—both Annette and I. And we'll be at the airport."

A moment later, she had put the receiver back in its cradle and was beaming at Annette. "He's coming home."

"Whee!" Annette bounced happily on Uncle Archie's overstuffed rocker. "Start packing!"

"Not just yet, dear," Aunt Lila said with a smile.

"But why not? Once he gets here, we can leave for Arizona, can't we?"

"I'm afraid not." Aunt Lila looked mysterious.

"But why not? Is Uncle Archie stopping somewhere else before he comes home?" Annette asked.

"No. They'll be here tomorrow afternoon."

"They?" Annette gasped. Surprise and

something like alarm mingled on Annette's pretty face. "Who?"

"Your uncle is bringing an old friend, Jim Burnett, and Jim's daughter, Sandy, for a visit." Aunt Lila's eyes were warm. "Goodness! I haven't thought of Jim Burnett for years!"

"The name sounds familiar," Annette said, knitting her brows, "but I don't know why."

"Your father probably mentioned him many times. They were like brothers, practically brought up together. They served in the same outfit during the war. In fact, Archie just told me that the Burnetts stayed at your house one summer when you were only a little girl," Aunt Lila explained.

"Oh," Annette said faintly, "I'm not sure—I—I think I remember *something*. . . . Will they be staying long?"

Aunt Lila looked at her sharply. Annette was wearing a frown. Aunt Lila laid her hand on her niece's arm. There was gentle reproach in her voice as she said quietly, "They'll be welcome to stay just as long as they wish to. They're old and dear friends."

For just a short moment more, Annette looked unhappy. Then she leaned over swiftly and kissed her aunt's cheek. "I'm sorry, Aunt Lila. I'm a selfish, spoiled character. Arizona can wait. We'll show them around and have a wonderful time!"

"That's my girl! I'm sure Lisa will understand and have a place at the inn for us when we can come."

"Of course! I'll write her tonight. And maybe, if the Burnetts haven't seen Arizona, we'll take them with us to Pine Mesa. I'm sure they'd love to attend a Native American ceremony!" Annette's disappointment had vanished. She was full of plans now.

"They've probably seen Native American ceremonies before. They've been living in Oklahoma for quite a few years. But I'm sure the native people in Arizona have different traditions, histories, and ceremonies. It would be a treat," Aunt Lila said.

"What sort of a person is Mr. Burnett?" Annette asked. "I can't seem to place him."

"A big man, with a loud sort of voice and full of fun. He did something around oil fields, so I guess he had to shout to be heard over the machinery or something! Mrs. Burnett was very delicate, with pale blond hair like a cloud. I saw her only once, when she and Jim were married. Poor lamb, she's gone now."

"I wonder—" Annette said, with a puzzled look. "I remember a little girl I played with a long time ago. She had that kind of hair, and so did her mother. That must have been the Burnetts." It was coming back to her now. She laughed suddenly. "I remember now. I was jealous of her because I heard Mom tell Dad one morning that Sandy—yes, that was her name!—that Sandy looked like a darling little angel right off a Christmas tree. I cried a bucketful of tears and hung around Mom's neck, yowling, because I was afraid she was sorry Sandy wasn't her little girl instead of me!"

"Children get silly ideas sometimes," Aunt Lila agreed. "But their fears seem awfully real at the time."

Annette nodded soberly. "Mom tried to tell me it was all in my mind, but I wasn't sure. So the first chance I got, I stamped my foot into a mud puddle and splashed mud all over Sandy's face. Then I tried to pull her curls out by the roots! I really did!"

Aunt Lila was shocked. "Good gracious, child! That was a very naughty thing to do."

"Oh, Sandy never tattled about it. All she did was grab me and push my face down into the same mud puddle. And when I got over bawling, we began laughing at how funny we both looked, all streaked with mud. And after that we got along just fine, as far as I can remember." Annette smiled.

"And the grown-ups probably thought you were both little angels!" Aunt Lila said dryly.

"I guess so. The only thing I do remember very clearly was when they took Sandy away and we hung on to each other and bawled and screamed because she didn't want to go and I didn't want her to, either! Then they took a train somewhere."

"And now you'll be together again! Don't you wonder what she's like now?" Aunt Lila asked.

"She was taller than I was, I remember. So I guess she's tall and slender. I bet she's pretty, too. I can hardly wait to show her off to the kids." She snapped her fingers suddenly. "Why can't I invite all the gang, the ones who aren't already out of town, to meet her? Maybe on Sunday night for a cookout and dance on our patio! Jinks can bring his newest records, and—" Annette paused to catch her breath and Aunt Lila interrupted.

"Whoa, child! Here's the phone. Work it out yourself. You'll have to make all the arrangements without my help. I'm going to be too busy running around getting things ready for our guests to worry about *your* department! But keep it down to half a dozen, and not too many show-offs. Sandy may be shy with strangers."

It took several phone calls to get the guests lined up, but within an hour Annette had a handful of her closest friends looking forward to meeting Sandy Burnett. And if some of the girls weren't exactly enthusiastic about welcoming a new girl to their circle, the boys made up for it as soon as Annette mentioned Sandy's blond hair and blue eyes.

Annette drove her uncle's five-year-old car, a big sedan, to the airport the next afternoon.

Aunt Lila was as excited as Annette as they watched the giant jet plane approach the field. And by the time it had taxied into position to discharge its passengers, they were eagerly peering through the windows of the terminal ramp to catch their first glimpse of Uncle Archie and his guests.

The long, covered passageway was crowded with others waiting to greet friends, but Aunt Lila and Annette held their place determinedly. "They're turning off the motors. And there go the landing steps!" Everyone was shoving.

Annette's pretty face was flushed with excitement. "Isn't this fun? I can hardly wait. Bet I see Uncle Archie before you do!"

Now the passengers were streaming out of the giant plane and moving down the stairway.

"There he is!" Aunt Lila waved wildly,

older after all these years!" Jim Burnett's booming voice made half the people there turn to stare. He strode ahead to Lila and Annette, and before Aunt Lila realized his intention, he had thrown his arms around her in a bear hug.

"Jim Burnett! Let go of me this minute! All these people! Goodness!" Aunt Lila's cheeks were pink with embarrassment and she was flustered as she backed hurriedly out of the hug. But Annette could see that she wasn't really angry with Mr. Burnett.

"Prettiest gal in school when we were kids!" Burnett chuckled. Then he noticed Annette smiling at him. "Hey! This must be Annette, all grown up!"

He held out his arms, and Annette could see that he was about to give her one of those bear hugs, too. "Hello, Mr. Burnett! Welcome to California!" she said, hastily shaking his hand.

"And, Lila, this is Jim's little girl, Sandy." Uncle Archie brought up Sandy, the tall girl still holding on to his arm as if she were afraid to let go. "Sandy—Aunt Lila."

although she knew Uncle Archie couldn't possibly see her yet.

Annette stared, standing on tiptoe. "I see him now! Is that Mr. Burnett—the big man behind Uncle Archie?"

"I guess it is. It's been so long—why, yes, it must be Jim. See, they're talking!" Aunt Lila exclaimed.

"But where's Sandy? Which one of those girls do you think is Sandy?"

"I'm sure I don't know, dear, any more than you do! But Uncle Archie said she would be with them, so perhaps she's that one, or *that* one." She nodded toward a couple of young women appearing in the doorway now.

"We'll soon know. Uncle Archie and Mr. Burnett are waiting at the foot of the stairs." Annette strained to watch. "Here come some more."

"They're all bunched together." Aunt Lila squinted uncertainly and adjusted her glasses. "I can't pick her out yet. You say she's a blonde, and there are several with light hair."

"I know which one it isn't!" Annette giggled. "The one in the gorgeous mink wrap. Even from here, I can tell she's a movie star or on the stage." Annette looked about quickly. "I wonder where the cameramen and reporters are?"

Aunt Lila gripped her arm suddenly. "Look!"

Startled, Annette stared at the landing steps. The tall, slim figure in the extravagant mink wrap had come down, stepping gingerly on four-inch high heels, and now she was turning to Uncle Archie and Jim Burnett, who were waiting there.

A moment later, all three were walking arm in arm toward the exit where Aunt Lila and Annette stood in speechless amazement, staring at them.

2   *Annette's Problem*

"Oh, dear!" Aunt Lila stared doubtfully at the tall girl on high heels and bundled in a costly mink wrap, tottering along between Uncle Archie and Jim Burnett. "I hardly expected—I mean, do you think that could be Sandy? That girl looks a lot older than Sandy would, I'm sure. It's probably someone they met on the plane."

But Annette had recovered quickly from her first surprise, and now as the trio came closer, she could see the light blond hair and the upturned nose that were familiar to her even after so long a time. "No, that's Sandy all right. And if you look so shocked, she'll be sure to notice."

"I'm sorry," Aunt Lila said hastily. "I wouldn't want to make her feel strange." She waved a welcoming hand at the three. "Archie! Here we are!"

"Lila! Pretty as ever and you don't look a day

"Hello, Aunt Lila," Sandy said, with surprising shyness.

Aunt Lila put out her hand mechanically. But in spite of her effort to speak cordially, her voice was not nearly as warm as she tried to make it, as she said, "We're very glad to have you with us, Sandy." She couldn't quite hide her dismay as her eyes swept quickly over Sandy's heavy makeup and her very extravagant clothing. It was undoubtedly what the fashion magazines called "high style," but it was too sophisticated for a girl of Sandy's age.

Annette saw Sandy's chin go up and noticed that she dropped Aunt Lila's hand after the briefest touch. And Sandy's "thank you" was cold and distant.

Aunt Lila realized at once that she had hurt Sandy's feelings, and she cast a quick look of appeal to Annette.

Annette decided it was time to step in. "Hi, Sandy!" she said quickly, with a friendly grin. "Remember your mud-puddle pal?" She held out both hands to her guest in an impulsive gesture.

Sandy melted at once. "Hi, Annette! Sure I do! Golly, I've thought of you so often and wished I could see you again." She took Annette's hands, and they stood beaming at each other. "I can hardly believe it's really coming true!"

"Well, here we are!" Annette laughed. "And won't we have a million things to talk about!"

"Sure will!" Sandy was beaming now.

Jim Burnett's voice interrupted. "And what do you think of my girl, Lila? Isn't she the grand little lady?"

"Yes, indeed," Aunt Lila answered quickly.

"Oh, Dad! You shouldn't say such things!" Sandy spoke sharply, her face flushing.

"Why not?" Jim Burnett boomed, wearing a wide grin. "It's what I think. And I plan to see to it from now on that my girl's right out in front with the best of them. Nobody's going to be able to look down on my Sandy. She's going to have everything anybody else has!"

"Dad!" Sandy raised her voice. People were staring at Jim Burnett. "Hadn't we better pick up our baggage?"

although she knew Uncle Archie couldn't possibly see her yet.

Annette stared, standing on tiptoe. "I see him now! Is that Mr. Burnett—the big man behind Uncle Archie?"

"I guess it is. It's been so long—why, yes, it must be Jim. See, they're talking!" Aunt Lila exclaimed.

"But where's Sandy? Which one of those girls do you think is Sandy?"

"I'm sure I don't know, dear, any more than you do! But Uncle Archie said she would be with them, so perhaps she's that one, or *that* one." She nodded toward a couple of young women appearing in the doorway now.

"We'll soon know. Uncle Archie and Mr. Burnett are waiting at the foot of the stairs." Annette strained to watch. "Here come some more."

"They're all bunched together." Aunt Lila squinted uncertainly and adjusted her glasses. "I can't pick her out yet. You say she's a blonde, and there are several with light hair."

"I know which one it isn't!" Annette giggled. "The one in the gorgeous mink wrap. Even from here, I can tell she's a movie star or on the stage." Annette looked about quickly. "I wonder where the cameramen and reporters are?"

Aunt Lila gripped her arm suddenly. "Look!"

Startled, Annette stared at the landing steps. The tall, slim figure in the extravagant mink wrap had come down, stepping gingerly on four-inch high heels, and now she was turning to Uncle Archie and Jim Burnett, who were waiting there.

A moment later, all three were walking arm in arm toward the exit where Aunt Lila and Annette stood in speechless amazement, staring at them.

2   *Annette's Problem*

"Oh, dear!" Aunt Lila stared doubtfully at the tall girl on high heels and bundled in a costly mink wrap, tottering along between Uncle Archie and Jim Burnett. "I hardly expected—I mean, do you think that could be Sandy? That girl looks a lot older than Sandy would, I'm sure. It's probably someone they met on the plane."

But Annette had recovered quickly from her first surprise, and now as the trio came closer, she could see the light blond hair and the upturned nose that were familiar to her even after so long a time. "No, that's Sandy all right. And if you look so shocked, she'll be sure to notice."

"I'm sorry," Aunt Lila said hastily. "I wouldn't want to make her feel strange." She waved a welcoming hand at the three. "Archie! Here we are!"

"Lila! Pretty as ever and you don't look a day

older after all these years!" Jim Burnett's booming voice made half the people there turn to stare. He strode ahead to Lila and Annette, and before Aunt Lila realized his intention, he had thrown his arms around her in a bear hug.

"Jim Burnett! Let go of me this minute! All these people! Goodness!" Aunt Lila's cheeks were pink with embarrassment and she was flustered as she backed hurriedly out of the hug. But Annette could see that she wasn't really angry with Mr. Burnett.

"Prettiest gal in school when we were kids!" Burnett chuckled. Then he noticed Annette smiling at him. "Hey! This must be Annette, all grown up!"

He held out his arms, and Annette could see that he was about to give her one of those bear hugs, too. "Hello, Mr. Burnett! Welcome to California!" she said, hastily shaking his hand.

"And, Lila, this is Jim's little girl, Sandy." Uncle Archie brought up Sandy, the tall girl still holding on to his arm as if she were afraid to let go. "Sandy—Aunt Lila."

"Hello, Aunt Lila," Sandy said, with surprising shyness.

Aunt Lila put out her hand mechanically. But in spite of her effort to speak cordially, her voice was not nearly as warm as she tried to make it, as she said, "We're very glad to have you with us, Sandy." She couldn't quite hide her dismay as her eyes swept quickly over Sandy's heavy makeup and her very extravagant clothing. It was undoubtedly what the fashion magazines called "high style," but it was too sophisticated for a girl of Sandy's age.

Annette saw Sandy's chin go up and noticed that she dropped Aunt Lila's hand after the briefest touch. And Sandy's "thank you" was cold and distant.

Aunt Lila realized at once that she had hurt Sandy's feelings, and she cast a quick look of appeal to Annette.

Annette decided it was time to step in. "Hi, Sandy!" she said quickly, with a friendly grin. "Remember your mud-puddle pal?" She held out both hands to her guest in an impulsive gesture.

Sandy melted at once. "Hi, Annette! Sure I do! Golly, I've thought of you so often and wished I could see you again." She took Annette's hands, and they stood beaming at each other. "I can hardly believe it's really coming true!"

"Well, here we are!" Annette laughed. "And won't we have a million things to talk about!"

"Sure will!" Sandy was beaming now.

Jim Burnett's voice interrupted. "And what do you think of my girl, Lila? Isn't she the grand little lady?"

"Yes, indeed," Aunt Lila answered quickly.

"Oh, Dad! You shouldn't say such things!" Sandy spoke sharply, her face flushing.

"Why not?" Jim Burnett boomed, wearing a wide grin. "It's what I think. And I plan to see to it from now on that my girl's right out in front with the best of them. Nobody's going to be able to look down on my Sandy. She's going to have everything anybody else has!"

"Dad!" Sandy raised her voice. People were staring at Jim Burnett. "Hadn't we better pick up our baggage?"

"I just saw it go by on the truck," Archie McCleod said hastily. "We can claim it now."

"Great! Let's get moving!" Jim Burnett took Aunt Lila's arm and started toward the sign that pointed to the baggage room. Uncle Archie hurried along with them, but Annette and Sandy stood silent a moment. Burnett's voice came back to them, "Wait till you see some of the fancy duds we picked up for Sandy in Tulsa. They'll knock your eyes out, sure enough!"

A couple of well-dressed men exchanged amused looks as they passed the girls, and Annette saw Sandy glare at them. But as she laid her hand on Sandy's arm and was about to start after the others, Sandy shook off the hand and faced her squarely.

"I know what some people think. They call Dad a loudmouth. But he isn't! He's a darling! And I—oh, never mind! Come on!"

Before Annette could say anything in reply, Sandy was stalking off after her father and the others, her high heels clicking angrily on the cement floor.

All Annette could do was to hurry after her, a little annoyed. Jeepers! she thought. She certainly has a chip on her shoulder about her dad. But maybe it was only because she wanted everybody to like her father and was afraid they wouldn't realize that he still hadn't gotten over the excitement of striking it rich in the oil fields. Aunt Lila had been telling Annette as they drove to the terminal that Jim Burnett's oil well had "come in" only a few months earlier, after many years of what they called "wildcatting."

Annette hadn't had a very clear idea until then of what wildcatting was, but Aunt Lila had explained that it meant going to places where no one else had found oil, and gambling time and money to try to find some there. Most of the wildcat wells were never successful, even after thousands and thousands of dollars had been sunk in them. Jim Burnett, according to Uncle Archie, had tried for years to locate a new oil field. He had organized company after company and had put every last cent into the exploration of possible locations. But until a few months ago, every well had been dry, and he had been forced to start over each time with empty pockets and only his hopes to keep him going.

Then, suddenly, on the brink of a new disappointment and down to his last penny, he had struck a gusher. And now he was rich, very rich. Money was flowing into his pockets as fast as oil was gushing out of the test well, and he had leased the rest of the field to a big oil company.

As the girls came up to the baggage desk, expensive new bags were piled high around Jim Burnett, and he was still claiming other pieces as half a dozen smiling porters clustered around him.

As the porters trotted off with the bags toward the parking area, Jim Burnett swaggered over to Aunt Lila. "Pretty slick, hey, Lila? Most expensive baggage I could find in the whole state! Paid a mint for it!" He caught Sandy's eye and winked mischievously. "Didn't we, honey?"

"We sure did, Dad!" Sandy said in a much louder voice than natural. And she glared defiantly at several passersby who had heard and smiled at the words.

But when Jim Burnett and the McCleods had started away after the porters, Sandy dropped her defiant air. Annette noticed how her shoulders drooped under the expensive fur wrap.

"Don't you feel well, Sandy? Is there anything I can do?" Annette said with sympathy.

Sandy seemed to hesitate a moment before she answered, as if she were tempted to explain. Then she shrugged her shoulders and laughed. "Why, no, thanks. I feel okay. Just tired, that's all."

But as they moved away toward the car, she was coldly silent, and she trotted along on her high heels so fast that it was all Annette could do to keep up with her, much less carry on a conversation.

Annette wanted to say something amusing to her, to bring back the friendly Sandy she had glimpsed for such a short moment when they first met, but she couldn't think of what to say with Sandy suddenly so abrupt. So she decided to keep quiet, and they reached the car in silence.

But by the time the heavily loaded car, with

Archie McCleod, Jim Burnett, and Aunt Lila in the front seat, had started the ride homeward, the two girls were at ease again. Annette pointed out places of interest as the car went down the main boulevard, and Sandy scanned them eagerly.

"We'll really have a ball taking in all the sights," Annette promised. "There are so many things to show you. And I know you'll love my gang from school. Some of them are dropping by Sunday night to meet you."

"Oh," Sandy replied timidly. She seemed about to say something, but stopped and stared out the window instead.

Now what's wrong? Annette wondered. The unpleasant thought came into her mind that maybe Sandy was trying to be snooty. Those expensive clothes—all that money rolling in—maybe she thought the gang wouldn't be swell enough!

But almost the moment the thought came, Annette dismissed it. Sandy isn't like that, she told herself firmly. It must be something else. I'll just leave her alone and she'll get over it.

So, for the last few minutes of the ride, Annette sat quietly and Sandy continued to stare out of the car window without speaking.

And even when Annette showed her into the pretty bedroom they had prepared for her, Sandy had little to say except that it was very nice.

"We thought you'd like this view of the hills," Annette told her, drawing aside the curtains of the north window. "This time of day they take on all sorts of colors."

For the first time since she had arrived, Sandy's face glowed with interest as she stared at the distant hills, now purple and dark blue with sunset shadows. "How lovely!" She caught her breath, then impulsively turned to Annette. "Can we climb them some day? I'd love to. It's been so long since we've lived anyplace but flat country and oil fields."

"We'll do it next week! Maybe have a picnic on top of Baldy Peak. We'll pack lunches and wear hiking shoes and slacks. And I'll see how many of the kids would like to go along," Annette said excitedly.

But the cloud had come over Sandy's face again. Turning away from the window, she answered, "That'll be nice." But she didn't sound very enthusiastic.

Annette started toward the door. "I'd better let you get settled," she said quietly. "I guess you're tired and want to rest before dinner."

"Thank you," Sandy said, and turned to stare out the window again.

"If there's anything you want, just yell and I'll get it for you." Annette was making an effort to keep her voice friendly and casual.

"Thank you." Sandy's voice was polite but not very friendly. "Everything's fine."

Annette hesitated a moment more, but Sandy kept her back turned, and Annette went out, closing the door behind her without another word.

In one of the big bedrooms down the hall, she could hear the two men's voices. Uncle Archie and Mr. Burnett were talking about the weather in cheerful voices.

Mr. Burnett seemed to approve of California. "Yes, sir!" he was saying heartily. "Always dreamed I'd hit it big some day and end up in sunny California with my girl. And, well, here we are!"

Annette went slowly downstairs. She felt sure that Mr. Burnett would be happy here, but she wasn't at all sure about Sandy. Sandy seemed to have a problem, and it looked as if it might turn into a problem for Annette, too!

3   *A Helping Hand*

Aunt Lila was busy preparing dinner in the kitchen when Annette came down from Sandy's room. Annette closed the hall door behind her slowly. She had a little frown on her face.

"I hope she liked the room," Aunt Lila said, smiling.

"She said everything was fine," answered Annette, still frowning, "but she didn't act like it." She went on to explain how Sandy had frozen up a couple of times when she, Annette, had made plans. "But I don't know why. I wish I did. Maybe I could help her."

"It's probably nothing serious, dear. Still, I wish she'd be more friendly. Then you could hint to her that her clothes are all wrong for a girl her age. And that theatrical makeup on her face—"

"She must have other clothes, Aunt Lila, for every day," Annette replied.

"Then I hope she wears them! And *lots* less makeup."

"But, Aunt Lila—" Annette stopped abruptly at the click of high heels in the hall beyond the closed door. "Here she comes now. Please, make believe you don't notice anything wrong with the way she looks," she whispered.

But the heel clicks sounded farther away now, and when Annette hurried to open the door, she caught only a glimpse of Sandy turning up the stairway at the other end of the hall. A moment later, the heels scurried along the upper hall, and Sandy's door closed with a bang.

Annette felt sick as she turned back, white-faced, to Aunt Lila. "She must have come to the door while you were talking, and we didn't hear her. And she must have heard what you said about her clothes."

"Oh, I hope not!" Aunt Lila looked stricken. "I didn't really mean to criticize. I just stated the truth. Do you think I should go up and apologize?"

Annette shook her head soberly. "I think I'd

better go. She's probably furious and will blow up, but I'll wait till she gets over it, and then I'll explain. And if she throws anything at me, I'll duck." She grinned reassuringly and dashed out into the hall, leaving Aunt Lila almost on the verge of tears over her unguarded criticism of their guest.

Annette hurried up the stairs toward Sandy's bedroom, wondering what she was going to say to her. By the time she had reached the closed door, she had decided that telling the truth was the best thing to do. The truth was that Aunt Lila thought Sandy's clothes weren't just right. And she would have to admit that she didn't think so either, even if Sandy did become angry and decide to throw the contents of all twelve suit-cases and bags at her.

She paused, with her hand raised to knock. A distinct sob came from inside the room. A gentle little sob that didn't sound at all angry.

Impulsively, Annette opened the door without knocking and stood in the doorway, looking at the spectacle of a bed piled high with half-unpacked bags of frilly lace, silk and satin gowns, heaps of lace-trimmed lingerie, and dozens of slippers in a rainbow of hues. And in the midst of it all was Sandy, face down and sobbing heartbrokenly.

"Sandy, honey!" Annette ran to her as Sandy, suddenly aware of her, rolled over and sat up, glaring.

"Go away! I'm getting out of here just as soon as I talk to my dad!" Mascara was streaked down her cheeks.

"Please, Sandy, listen to me," Annette pleaded.

"I *did* listen. I didn't mean to. I only wanted to come and talk to you about something. And I heard what you think about me! Go away!" She covered her face and sobbed.

Annette's eyes flashed. At least Sandy could let her explain. "Sandy, stop crying! I'm your friend, and so is Aunt Lila." She spoke sharply to jolt Sandy out of her tears.

Sandy looked up, sniffling. "It didn't sound like it!"

Annette sat down on the edge of the bed. "All

right, so Aunt Lila and I don't like your clothes. They honestly aren't right."

For a moment, Sandy was silent. Then she said in a subdued little voice, "I know. I knew it the minute I saw you at the plane. And the other girls there—none of them had on fancy things like mine. I knew right away I looked like a freak."

"Not a freak, Sandy," Annette said, putting her arm around the girl. "Just too dressed up." She touched Sandy's mascara-streaked cheek with a light finger and showed the black smudge on it to Sandy. "And too painted up."

"It was those snippy salesladies in the dress shops," Sandy told Annette, holding her hand tightly. "They told Dad that everybody in Hollywood wore clothes like this, and I'd just have to look as good as they did or they'd laugh at me, even if we did have lots of money. So Dad bought just about everything they showed him. He didn't want folks out here to suspect we'd been poor before."

"But you must have some plainer things—"

Sandy shook her head unhappily. "I gave them all away. Dad insisted. Annette, what am I going to do? I can't meet your friends all dolled up in this fluff. They'll laugh at me."

"No, they won't," Annette told her, but even to herself she didn't sound very convincing. "They're nice kids."

"I wouldn't blame them!" Sandy said darkly. "If only the stores weren't closed, we could do some fast shopping before the gang gets here tomorrow evening." Annette started picking up one dress after the other and laying them all aside as hopeless. "Maybe you could wear my things."

"Your skirt would hit me four inches above the knees!" Sandy grinned and then looked gloomy. "Darn!"

"Hey, look. This fussy suit with the braided jacket! The skirt's perfectly plain. I'll lend you one of my blouses or sweater sets to go with it. That's what the others will be wearing. Nobody dresses up on Sunday night. We'll be sitting around the floor, playing records most likely."

"Oh, Annette, that will be marvelous!"

They hugged each other, laughing happily. And a few minutes later, after much scurrying back and forth between their rooms, and some face scrubbing that took off most of Sandy's mascara and eyeliner, the two went downstairs arm in arm.

Aunt Lila stared, surprised, at Sandy's pert little face with its small amount of makeup. "My goodness, child, you look like a different girl! Come here and let me see how pretty you are!"

And when Sandy shyly stepped close, Aunt Lila took her in her arms, and with Annette looking on approvingly, kissed her cheek. Then she let go of her and, pretending to be stern, told them, "Scoot, both of you, and start setting the table. Might as well break you in right away, Sandy. Annette, show her which silver we use for the family."

And when the girls had hurried off, Aunt Lila listened to their giggles as they fussed with the table setting. She was happy and relieved that Annette had smoothed things over.

Sandy still seemed to have panicky moments the next day as she and Annette looked forward to the evening.

"Do you think they'll like me—really?" she asked several times. "I've never had a chance to make any real friends, living all around, first in one little oil town and then another. But I've always wanted to."

"They'll think you're wonderful! Just be yourself. And, please, show them those old canvas sneakers you had on the morning your father's well came in. They'll get the biggest kick out of how you stood out in the field with the oil pouring down from the oil rig till you were sopping wet from it!"

"Oh, they might think I was trying to remind them of Dad's money, don't you think?" Sandy objected shyly.

Annette shook her head. "No, they won't. They're not like that."

And they weren't. They took to Sandy at once and laughed heartily at her account of the great morning when the gusher came in. And they all admired the disreputable-looking, oil-soaked sneakers that Sandy had held on to as a precious souvenir.

And by the time Aunt Lila finally shooed them home, they had all told Annette how much they liked Sandy and hoped she would be around a long time.

It was Teeny Travers who stopped in the doorway to ask Sandy and Annette, "How about a ride up to the lake in the morning? There's a whole gang going from Quigley's at eight o'clock, and it ought to be fun."

Sandy looked at Annette and nodded eagerly. Annette smiled at Teeny. "You've got a couple of customers."

"Okay, then. We'll look for you, but don't be too late. We want to get there before the sun gets hot. The boys want to do some jumping," Teeny explained.

"We'll be there at eight on the dot," Annette assured her, and Teeny dashed off to a waiting car.

"Is it far to this lake?" Sandy asked as the door closed after the visitors.

"Just a few miles. But the last part, before you get to the top, is pretty tough going. The horses can't go very fast."

"Horses?" Sandy looked surprised. "I thought we were going in cars."

It was Annette's turn to look surprised and worried.

"Don't you ride?" she asked Sandy.

"I've never tried, but I'm sure I can."

"Sure you can?" Annette repeated. "Well, you're not going to break your neck trying to learn on that steep bridle path! I'll call Teeny early in the morning and tell her to go on without us."

"No!" Sandy said sharply. "I'll be all right. Please don't say anything."

Annette stared at her unbelievingly. And Sandy met her eyes stubbornly. "But why not? It's no disgrace not to be able to ride a horse!" Annette exclaimed.

"I said I'd go, and I'm going. Will you lend me something to wear?"

Annette hesitated another minute; then she held

up her hands in surrender. "Okay. I have some jeans that'll fit you. And wear your sneakers."

But long before daylight, Annette was wide awake and worrying. And by six o'clock she had roused Sandy out of a peaceful sleep and had her dressed and down in the kitchen, drinking a hurried cup of cocoa and nibbling on a bun.

A few minutes later, they were speeding toward Quigley's stable in Annette's neat little white Monster.

It was a very sleepy groom who brought out two horses for them, grumbling about people who said eight o'clock and came before seven, expecting service.

When he had shuffled away, Annette made one last effort to change Sandy's mind. "Please, don't take a chance of getting hurt," she pleaded.

But Sandy was determined to go through with it.

"All right, then," Annette agreed. "I'll show you how to mount." And she demonstrated for Sandy, explaining as she went.

"It looks easy," Sandy told her, as Annette

dismounted after an easy canter across the ring and back.

"Try it," Annette told her. "Reins in your hand, like this—other hand on the saddle here. Now the left foot in the stirrup. Up and over."

Sandy obeyed eagerly and did everything exactly right.

"Good!" Annette congratulated her.

"It's kind of high up here, isn't it?" There was a tremor in Sandy's voice as she looked down at Annette.

"You'll get used to it." Annette laughed. "Now hang on till I mount old Chief, and we'll ride around a little."

They were still at it when the others came drifting in.

The horses were ready and they mounted expertly and set out, laughing and chatting back and forth.

Annette waited deliberately and held Sandy back.

"How do you feel by now?" she asked. "We can still back out. I can tell Teeny I have a headache and nobody'll think anything of our not going."

"Oh, Annette! Stop worrying! I'm doing fine, and I don't want to miss the fun."

So Annette rode with her after the others, but she couldn't help worrying. If anything happened, she would never forgive herself for letting Sandy go along.

4   *A Tumble*

The bridle path to Sunset Lake started out at an easy level through a parklike grove of tall sycamores and oaks, but it wasn't long before it began to get steep.

The young riders were spread out, some riding alone and others in pairs. Teeny was in the lead and setting the pace, though Annette usually did it.

Annette had made a point of bringing up the rear with Sandy, so she could keep an eye on her. Her excuse was that she wanted to point out scenery to her guest.

At first, Sandy seemed to be enjoying herself, but it wasn't long before Annette could see that she was getting tired and hanging on to the reins with a tight grip of both hands.

Ahead, Teeny called a halt at the foot of a steep side trail. There seemed to be a debate going on among the riders.

"Uh-oh! She wants to take the shortcut! It's steep and rocky. I hope they vote her down," Annette said with a frown.

Sandy moved uncomfortably in her saddle. Her strained muscles were beginning to tire. "I'm voting for the short one, steep or not!" she cried. "I'm beginning to fall apart at the seams!"

Annette was tempted to say, "I tried to warn you!" but she bit back the words. Sandy already knew it, and it seemed almost like gloating, which was something Annette disliked. Instead, as she saw Teeny up ahead turn toward the start of the steeper trail, she laughed a little grimly and said, "Looks as if you'll get your wish. She's taking the short way."

"We can't get there soon enough for me," Sandy said with a groan. "I'm finding out about a lot of muscles I never knew I had till now!"

As they came to the trail where the rest of the party had disappeared, they could hear the others urging their horses up the narrow way, and little showers of loosened stones were still falling.

Sandy's horse seemed unwilling to start up. "Now what?" she asked uneasily.

"Sit tight and give him his head," Annette told her. "If you pull back on the reins, you might topple him back on yourself. Start up, and I'll follow closely—just in case."

So they started up the trail, and to Annette's relief there were no stumbles. Trusty Eagle, Sandy's horse, never faltered once.

By the time they reached the broad grassy stretch of picnic grounds beside the mountain lake, Sandy was feeling quite sure of herself.

"It wasn't too scary," Sandy said to Annette as they rode toward the spot where the other girls were getting one of the picnic tables dusted off. "Riding a horse isn't so hard to do, once you get used to it."

Annette nodded, but she smiled to herself as she looked away. Sandy was just lucky that she hadn't been taking her first ride on a high-spirited horse instead of old Eagle. Any horse can sense, the moment a rider is in the saddle, just how much the person knows about handling the mount. And some of them give a green rider a bad time by acting skittish or stubborn.

She was glad she had tipped off the groom at Quigley's to assign the steadiest horse in the stables to Sandy.

"What are they doing over there?" Sandy asked, nodding toward a spot beside the lake where a couple of the boys were setting up what looked like a low wooden gate.

"They're going to practice jumping," Annette explained. "Watch Teeny's brother. He's very good."

One of the young men had mounted and was riding rapidly toward the other end of the green. He wheeled suddenly and came cantering back toward the barrier. A moment later, rider and horse rose into the air and soared gracefully over it, landing safely on the other side.

Annette and the others cheered as he cantered back to try the barrier at a higher setting. He pulled in and made a mock bow to them before he rode to the other end of the grassy stretch.

One of the boys ran out to lift the bars to a

higher notch while the rider waited for the path to be clear.

No one paid any attention to a small boy on a bicycle who had arrived to watch. The brown dog that had been running alongside the boy strained at the rope that the boy held in his hand. "All right, King, go get a drink if you want it," the small boy told him, and slipped off the dog's rope collar. The dog ran toward the lake.

Annette and Sandy were still in their saddles, watching admiringly as Teeny's brother got ready to start his second run at the barrier. Neither noticed the brown dog stop to sniff at Eagle's heels. But Eagle noticed.

He kicked out at the dog, and the animal gave a yip of pain. Before Sandy knew what was happening, the dog had nipped Eagle on the fetlock, and the big horse had started off across the grass on the run.

All Sandy could do was hang on to the pommel and Eagle's mane. One foot came out of the stirrup, and she slipped around in the saddle.

Teeny's brother had already started toward the barrier at a full gallop. He was intent on the jump and didn't even notice the big horse that was heading his way.

In a glance, Annette saw that the two horses would probably get to the same spot at the same time. She nudged her horse into motion and rode desperately to overtake Eagle and try to grab the flying reins to stop him in time.

Now Teeny's brother saw the danger and tried to slow his horse, but it was moving too fast.

Eagle galloped across the path of the jumper, but just as he cleared, Sandy fell out of the saddle and landed on her hands and knees.

Annette swept toward her while the boys yelled and the girls screamed. Sandy was scrambling to her feet now, and the galloping jumper was headed straight for her, moving fast in spite of his rider's effort to slow him.

But while he was still some distance away from the dazed girl, the boy managed to turn him at an angle, and it seemed certain that he would miss Sandy by a safe margin.

At the last minute, she saw him coming and broke into a run, trying to get clear. Instead, she ran into his path again and stood there, dazed.

The horrified rider pulled back on the reins and shouted, but the horse was confused now at the sudden changes in direction, and it fought the bit and kept coming.

Annette swept in to where Sandy stood helpless. "Sandy! Grab my arm and hang on!" she yelled as she pulled up to a sliding stop. And as Sandy mechanically obeyed and grasped Annette's extended arm, Annette closed her fist in a tight grip on Sandy's sleeve and kicked her horse into motion again.

They were clear by less than a yard as the big jumper swept by. Annette could feel the swish of his tail as he passed.

She rode a short distance and then let go of Sandy. Sandy tumbled to the grass and sat there, looking completely bewildered. Annette's arm felt as if it had been pulled out of its socket, but she ignored it as she dismounted hastily and ran back to Sandy.

Sandy was only shaken up, but as Annette helped her to her feet, she was on the verge of tears. "I'm sorry, Annette. It was all my fault for trying to make believe I could ride. You might have gotten hurt trying to save me!"

Annette saw the others all running to find out what had caused the near accident. "Nonsense!" she said, a little sharply to make Sandy snap out of it. "A runaway like that could happen to anybody."

And when Teeny and the others arrived, full of questions and condolences, Annette laughed it all off.

"That brown dog trotting so peacefully down the road with the little boy started the whole thing!" she said with a laugh, nodding after the pair. "He nipped old Eagle, and Eagle went on the warpath."

"I never saw him go faster than a trot before," one of the boys said with a laugh. "It's a good thing Annette hadn't dismounted!"

"How did you happen to lose the reins?" Teeny asked Sandy.

Sandy looked startled and puzzled. The last time she had seen Eagle, his reins were still attached to his bridle, even though they were flipping wildly in the air. Why did Teeny say that she had *lost* them?

"I'm afraid I don't know what you—" she began to say, with a glance in Annette's direction that said plainly, "Help!"

Annette caught the look and interrupted cheerfully. "Let's talk about it after Sandy's had a cup of hot chocolate and stopped shaking."

"Oh, of course!" Teeny said contritely. "I'll get it ready right away." And she hurried off toward the picnic table.

Annette linked her arm with Sandy's and started after Teeny as the others scattered. Teeny's brother rode after old Eagle to bring him back.

"What did Teeny mean about losing the reins?" Sandy asked with a frown.

"She meant 'lose hold of them,' not actually *lose* them," Annette said with a grin. "It's just a riding expression. You'll learn a lot of them."

Sandy shook her head. "It's no use! I'm going to tell them all, right now, that I never learned to ride. I'm sorry I was so stubborn about it and tried to fool myself and everybody else."

Annette could see that she really meant to do it. "I suppose you'd better," Annette agreed reluctantly.

"They're bound to find out, anyhow," Sandy said glumly.

But Annette snapped her fingers suddenly and laughed. "No, they won't! Because next time anybody says, 'Let's go for a ride!' you'll be ready and willing!"

Sandy looked bewildered. "How?"

"Tomorrow morning you and I have a date at Quigley's stables, and *you're* going to take riding lessons!"

Sandy's face was radiant. "Oh, Annette! You're the best friend I've ever had! I'll learn fast, honestly. You'll be proud of me next time."

"I'd better be!" Annette said with playful sternness.

Sandy grinned happily. Then, with sudden inspiration, she told Annette, "The very first thing I'm going to do tonight is make Dad promise we'll stay out here on the Coast all summer. And I'm going to get him to buy a nice big house right near yours so we can be together when school opens."

"That's a super idea!" Annette agreed.

"I'll try to pin him down to it at dinner tonight," Sandy told her happily, "and you can help."

"You can count on me," Annette assured her.

But big Jim Burnett had already decided that he, too, would like living in Southern California. He had spent most of the day with Uncle Archie and a real estate dealer.

"Got a line on just the kind of place we're going to want to live in," he told Sandy at the dinner table. "Soon as my new car's delivered tomorrow morning, we'll go look it over."

"Oh, Dad! That's wonderful!" Sandy threw a delighted glance toward Annette.

"What part of town is it in, Jim?" Aunt Lila asked.

"Well, it isn't exactly in town. It's about a hundred miles up the coast, at a place called Moonstone Bay."

5   *Moonstone Bay*

"A hundred miles away?" Sandy repeated, shocked. Her eyes met Annette's in a silent appeal.

"Oh," Annette said quickly, "we were hoping you'd want to live down here, Mr. Burnett."

"Two hours isn't far away," Jim Burnett said with a chuckle, "and from what I hear, this Moonstone Bay's got everything. The place we're going to look at is right on the shore. Two and a half acres, sixteen-room house, private stable—the whole works."

"It's the old Glaven place," Uncle Archie explained to Aunt Lila.

"Why, I've been there on one of the Garden Tours," Aunt Lila said. "It's lovely! The rose garden's a hundred years old, they told us. And the original adobe house is still standing, though no one lives there now."

"It sounds icky to me!" Sandy suddenly exploded.

Her father looked startled, and Annette hurriedly covered a grin with her napkin. Sandy's eyes were stormy as she went on. "I don't want to live a hundred miles away. I want to live right around here and be with Annette."

Jim Burnett frowned. "I looked at a couple of places, but it seems like there's nothing for sale down here that's as good."

"But there must be!" Sandy argued. "And I don't even want to go and look at that place!"

"Honey, we haven't bought it yet. Maybe we'll end up near here, after all, but we're going to look at the Moonstone Bay place first. I let the real estate man make a date for us with the owner for tomorrow afternoon, and I aim to keep it!" He looked severe and added, "Whether you come along or not."

Sandy hesitated, with a quick glance at Annette. Annette nodded, to her surprise, and smiled. Sandy was puzzled, but she turned back to her father, swallowed hard, and then said meekly, "All right, Dad. I guess I will go."

"That's a good girl!" Jim Burnett patted her hand.

"I think you'll like it," Aunt Lila said joyfully, "and, really, it's not too far away for you and Annette to see a lot of each other. It should be fun visiting back and forth."

A few minutes later, as the two girls carried dishes out to the kitchen, they paused there for hasty whispers.

"Why did you tell me to say I'd go?" Sandy asked.

"Because if you don't go, your dad will probably let them stick him with some big old white elephant of a place that's falling to pieces! You remember how he let the salesladies sell him all sorts of fancy clothes that were wrong for you!"

"I hadn't thought of that," Sandy said. "You're right, Annette. I'll go with him, and this time nobody's going to take advantage of Dad just because he's got scads of money all of a sudden."

"Good!" Annette agreed. "You can find a lot

of things you don't like about it, if he starts to weaken."

"You bet I will! I don't care if the place is Buckingham Palace for ten dollars. I'll still talk him out of it. We'll be back in twenty-four hours!"

"And start those riding lessons!" Annette laughed.

But two days passed with no word from Sandy. Then three days and four. And on the fifth day, as Annette packed to go to the beach house with Aunt Lila, the phone rang.

It was Sandy calling from a pay phone in San Benito, the small town near the Moonstone Bay colony.

"Annette! Please, you've got to come and help me! Dad won't listen to me! I'm sure he's going to buy the Glaven place if I don't think of some way to stop him. And, Annette, *I'm scared*!"

"Sandy!" She sounded so hysterical that Annette was almost annoyed with her. "Why on earth are you scared? That doesn't make sense!"

"But it does! Annette, please, come as soon as you can! I'll explain it all when you get here!" Sandy pleaded.

"Oh, Sandy! Calm down! I promised Aunt Lila I'd help her get the beach house cleaned up for company. I can't leave her with all the work."

"All right, then," Sandy said, sobbing, "I g-guess if you don't want to help me, that's okay." There was a sniff and "Good-bye!"

"Sandy, wait a minute! What hotel are you stopping at in San Benito?" Annette had given in.

"You mean you'll come?" Sandy's voice was joyful.

"I suppose so," Annette answered, a little crossly.

"Oh, golly! Thanks, Annette! We're not at a hotel. Dad and I are staying at Mrs. Glaven's house. She thought we could tell better how we'd like living here if we were guests for a few days. And now Dad's crazy about it and—when can you come?"

"I can't just come barging into a private home, Sandy. That's silly!"

"But I asked Mrs. Glaven if I could invite you, and she said yes. And then—oh, please, Annette, come as soon as you can! It's Eighty-four Channel Cove."

"Okay," Annette promised, "though I'm sure I don't know what good I can do. See you tomorrow afternoon around three."

Aunt Lila was disappointed that Annette wasn't going to the beach with her. "Well, I suppose the poor child needs you, or thinks that she does. What she needs is self-confidence. She must stop thinking that everyone is going to look down on her if she shows that she hasn't had all the advantages others may have had."

"I imagine that's it, Aunt Lila," Annette agreed. "I wonder, though, what she means by being *scared*?"

It was a lovely sunny day, and on the highway along the coast, Annette's shiny white Monster sped along past town after town till the red-tiled roofs of San Benito appeared. There she made a quick turn off the highway, down through twin ranks of towering eucalyptus trees, and along a wide beach road beside a cool green ocean dotted with white sails. Big estates rimmed the winding road now, each seeming more impressive than the previous one. Then, suddenly, she saw a mailbox marked GLAVEN and tall iron gates standing open at the foot of a winding driveway rimmed by myriads of blossoming geraniums of every shade of pink.

Annette slowed down and made the turn into the Glaven driveway. And as she did, a small black sports car came roaring down the driveway from the sprawling white mansion situated high on the wide green lawns.

She wrenched her wheel over hard to avoid a collision, but even so there was scarcely a foot between the sides of the two cars as the speedster hurtled by.

It happened so quickly that her only impression of the driver was that he was a scowling young man, broad-shouldered and sitting tall in the tiny car, and that he was wearing a red-and-white-striped car cap.

She sat for a minute, shaken by the very close call, before she could pull herself together and back off the crushed geraniums. In the distance, the sound of the sports car's powerful engine died away.

She drove slowly toward the mansion, angry and still trembling a little at her narrow escape from a bad accident.

She pulled up in front of the house and stopped. By the time she was out of the car and starting toward the door, it was flung open and Sandy came rocketing out.

"Annette! You did come!" Sandy flung her arms around Annette.

"I said I would, didn't I?" Annette returned the hug with warmth.

A dignified butler came out to get her bags, followed by a liveried chauffeur who prepared to take Annette's car. She turned over the keys and started toward the house with Sandy.

"By the way, who was that hurry-up character in the roadster who almost cracked into me as I was turning in?" Annette asked.

"I don't know"—Sandy spoke softly so the men would not hear—"but I have an idea why he came. Tell you later."

Mrs. Glaven was waiting to greet her latest guest, and there was no chance for Sandy to explain just then.

Annette had been speculating on the way up to Moonstone Bay about what Mrs. Glaven would be like. She was agreeably surprised. There certainly didn't seem to be anything about their hostess to suggest that she might be scary. She was younger than Annette had expected and quite charming. Her soft voice was tinged with a southern drawl.

"I'm so glad you could come and stay with us awhile," Mrs. Glaven told Annette as she took both her hands. "Sandy was beginning to get a little bored, I'm afraid. There aren't many young people around just now."

"Thank you, Mrs. Glaven." Annette smiled. "It's good of you to have me."

"I do have a little news for you girls, though." She picked up an envelope from a nearby table.

"This is for both of you." She handed the envelope to Sandy. "Do read it."

Sandy took it reluctantly, and Annette saw a frown appear on her forehead as she read the engraved card that had been enclosed. Then, without a word, she handed the card to Annette.

"Oh!" Annette's eyes sparkled. "A fox hunt! And a ball afterward! That sounds exciting!"

"I thought you'd like the idea. It's really one of our top events of the season, and there couldn't be a better chance for Sandy to meet the people who will be her neighbors, *if* her dear father decides that he wishes this to be his home." She smiled. "I do so hope he will!"

Annette saw Sandy stiffen at the mention of her father, and she put her hand warningly on Sandy's arm.

"I'm afraid we'll have to send regrets," Annette told Mrs. Glaven. "I didn't bring a riding habit. Did you, Sandy?"

Sandy shook her head sullenly. But Mrs. Glaven gave a little laugh as she told them, "I'll

take you to the best tailor in San Benito tomorrow morning. He'll outfit both of you in time, *if*
you want him to." She looked troubled suddenly.
"You do like to ride, don't you?" The question
was addressed to both of them.

"Love it!" Annette agreed, but Sandy bit her
lower lip and didn't answer.

"Your father has ordered his outfit already,"
Mrs. Glaven told Sandy. "He's like a child with
a new toy. He tells me he hasn't ridden since he
was a boy. We're going to practice every day till
the hunt."

Annette was glad that the butler came in just
then to say that the bags were in her room. She
and Sandy excused themselves and went up.

The moment that the door was closed, Sandy
burst out angrily, "You see? She's just determined to sell Dad this place, and every day he's
getting more and more convinced that he wants
to buy it!"

Annette had been looking around the beauti-
fully furnished bedroom with its separate
dressing room and its wide windows looking out

on a charming old rose garden. "But it's lovely, Sandy. And Mrs. Glaven is charming!"

Sandy scowled at her. "You wouldn't think so if you had heard her a few minutes ago, shouting at some fellow. And he was shouting right back at her. I don't know what it was all about, but he went out and slammed the door."

"Tall guy in a black sports car?" Annette demanded.

"I didn't see him," Sandy said crossly, "but I heard him say something about money. I guess he was one of the tradesmen from San Benito. Mary, the upstairs maid, told me yesterday that Mrs. Glaven owes everybody." She scoffed. "No wonder she's trying to unload this place on Dad. But she's *not* going to!"

"It looks as if she thinks she will," Annette said soberly. "Have you talked to him?"

"Over and over. He won't even listen when I talk now. He says it's no crime for her to need money. Annette, please, help me think of some way to get out of this! Some awful thing is going to happen if Dad buys this place!"

"Why on earth do you think a thing like that?" Annette asked.

"Here, read this!" Sandy took out a folded piece of writing paper from the pocket of her cardigan. "I found it slipped under my door yesterday morning!"

The note was crudely printed in pencil. It read:

WORD OF WARNING. JUSTICE WILL BE DONE. DO NOT BUY THIS HOUSE OR YOU WILL BE SORRY.

6 *The Black Stallion*

"It sounds like a joke to me!" Annette said lightly. "Somebody's playing tricks."

"I don't think so," Sandy told her solemnly.

Annette read out the words of the mysterious note with a slight giggle. "'Justice will be done!'" She made it sound even more melodramatic. "Oh, Sandy, you can't take a thing like this seriously. It's too, too corny! It just has to be a joke. Are there any kids living here who might get a kick out of scaring you?"

"There isn't one on the property," Sandy said stubbornly. "I tell you it's a threat. And whoever left that note lives right here, or they wouldn't have been able to slip it under my door."

Annette sobered. "If you really believe it's serious, you ought to show it to your father and get him to investigate."

"I showed it to him right away, but he

just laughed, the same as you're doing. He thinks it's only a joke, but—" Sandy hesitated, frowning.

"Has anything else happened that makes you so sure it isn't some kid trick?"

Sandy nodded slowly. "The way Mrs. Glaven acted when Dad showed this note to her. She called in all the staff from the butler to the chauffeur and accused each of them separately of trying to make 'more trouble' for her. That's what she said—'*more trouble.*'"

"If she owes as much money everywhere as the maid told you, maybe she owes them back wages and they've been bothering her about it," Annette proposed.

"But whoever wrote this note doesn't seem to want her to sell us the place, even though that would give her enough to settle up any amount of debts. It doesn't make sense to think one of them would overlook that," Sandy argued. "I'm all puzzled."

"What did they say when she accused them?"

"They were all angry. And poor old Mary,

who's been with the Glaven family for ages, broke down and cried."

"I guess it's no joke trying to keep things peaceful in a great big place like this," Annette said soberly.

"I'd be afraid to try," Sandy admitted. "I can't help feeling that people might not be very friendly. Of course, Mrs. Glaven tells Dad they'll all be delighted to have us for neighbors."

"Maybe they will be, Sandy," Annette told her. "Have you met many of the San Benitans?"

"Quite a few, and they seem nice enough. They're all quite well off and come from old families. But I'm afraid they'll think we're just upstarts from the oil fields, and they'll laugh at us behind our backs."

"I hope you didn't tell your dad that," Annette said seriously. "You'd certainly hurt his feelings."

"Oh, no!" Sandy said. "I wouldn't tell him. He's having such a good time."

"And I bet you'll find that both of you will get along fine!" Annette assured her.

But Sandy shook her head stubbornly.

A light knock on the door interrupted them. Mrs. Glaven's voice called, "Sandy!"

Sandy wrinkled her nose at Annette. "Come in, Mrs. Glaven."

"Don't let me interrupt, darlings," Peggy Glaven told them lightly, as she entered, "but your father has made an appointment for both of you, Sandy, at the tailor's. You're to choose the material for your new riding habits. Hanover's, tomorrow at ten. I'd go with you, but I'm sure you'll have more fun by yourselves."

When they had both thanked her politely, and she had told them where to find the tailor shop in San Benito, Peggy Glaven hurried away again, bubbly and content.

Annette was serious after the door closed behind their hostess. "Sandy, I'm worried," she said gravely. "The more I think of that fox hunt, the more it seems to me you'd be taking a chance of getting hurt if you tried to ride as hard and fast as you'd be expected to."

Sandy frowned. "Well, I'm not going to back

out and let these people around here know that I'm not used to riding a horse."

"Just plain riding's one thing," Annette told her gently, "but a fox hunt is different. You never know which way the fox will run. And you have to follow the dogs, even if it's up a hill or over a creek. It's dangerous."

But Sandy looked stubborn and shook her head. "I'll hang on somehow." And Annette couldn't talk her out of it.

"Of course," Annette said finally, "we have a whole week before the hunt. You and I could practice together every day. And maybe, by that time, you'll be able to keep up with most of the other riders. But I still think it's risky."

Sandy hugged her friend impulsively. "You're a doll! How soon can we get started?"

Annette laughed and threw up both of her hands in surrender. "Soon as we get back from the tailor shop tomorrow—that is, if you don't change your mind."

"Don't worry! I won't! It'll be you who'll change your mind when you see how fast I'll learn!" Sandy answered saucily. And Annette hoped that Sandy was right.

They told Mrs. Glaven at the dinner table about their plans to ride every day—"to sort of brush up a bit," Sandy told her hostess grandly.

"Splendid!" Mrs. Glaven nodded approvingly.

But Annette couldn't help worrying. She decided that she'd better make sure that they had good steady mounts, at least during Sandy's first practice sessions. "Which horses may we use?" she asked Mrs. Glaven.

"Take your choice of any that old Patrick, the head groom, recommends," Mrs. Glaven told her graciously.

"We'll ask him for well-behaved ones till we're better acquainted with the bridle trails around here."

"All my horses are well trained," Peggy Glaven assured her. Then she frowned suddenly. "With the exception of one. Black Prince has become quite vicious since my husband passed away. No one can ride him." She sighed.

Jim Burnett walked in, just in time to catch Mrs. Glaven's remark.

"I'd like to try, after I've had a few more days of practice. He's a handsome animal," Jim Burnett told her.

"Please, don't try!" she said sharply. "He's far too dangerous. In fact, I intend to sell him before he hurts anyone."

It was a beautiful morning that greeted Annette when she awoke in her sunny bedroom. She stretched luxuriously between the fine linen sheets and wondered what it would be like to be rich enough to live in a mansion like this all the time.

Through the open window the sound of an electric mower came from a distance, rhythmic and soothing. She was lazily dropping off to sleep again, when the clip-clop of hooves awoke her and took her hurriedly to the window to see who was out so early.

The two riders were Sandy's father and Mrs. Glaven. They were just going out the gate, Jim Burnett on a chestnut gelding and Mrs. Glaven looking very neat and trim on a small, dainty mare.

"Dad's doing all right, isn't he?" Sandy had come in without Annette hearing her. "He looks fine on a horse. I hope we can buy a place down near you where we can keep horses."

"I'm sure there are quite a few sections of town where most of the people have horses," Annette assured her. Then she asked lightly as they turned from the window, "Did anything spooky happen during the night?"

"Well, there weren't any more of those scary notes, but I did hear some funny noises that I couldn't figure out. And once it sounded like somebody was banging at that side window."

Annette looked toward the window quickly. One shutter was closed, but the other was open and swaying gently. She crossed the room and reached for the loose shutter. "Did it sound like this?" She pulled the shutter toward her and banged it a couple of times against the window frame.

"That's it!" Sandy laughed. "You should have been a 'deteckatif'!" But a moment later she said, pouting, "The whole house is rickety."

But Annette wouldn't agree. She pointed out that the place looked pretty elegant to her, and that even the paint both inside and out was fresh and new.

"It looks as if somebody's been spending a lot of money fixing up everything lately," she told Sandy.

"Sure," Sandy said sourly, "covering up the bad points so my Dad can be fooled into thinking he's getting a big bargain. The only reason Mrs. Glaven's being so nice to us is that nobody but Dad has nibbled at the bait." She scowled. "That's all the use she has for us."

Annette decided that Sandy was being a bit unfair. "You ought to get over feeling that way, if you can. Your dad's a fine person, and people like to have him around even if they aren't trying to pawn off something on him, don't they?"

Sandy hesitated a moment, frowning. Then she smiled and nodded. "Of course. Dad had lots of friends back home. It's just that—"

Annette finished it for her. "Just that you've

made up your mind not to like anything around here."

"It's partly that," Sandy admitted with her usual frankness, "but it's something else, too, that makes me feel uneasy. That note wasn't a joke. I'm sure of it. There's something going on."

The girls soon forgot their suspicions when they went into town after breakfast. There were many fascinating stores near the tailor's, and they shopped to their hearts' content and came back laden with so many packages that Sandy could hardly see over the tops of them as they drove homeward.

Mrs. Glaven and Sandy's father had returned from their ride and were the center of an energetic group of riders who had stopped off for a luncheon on the wide terrace behind the main house.

Mrs. Glaven introduced the girls to her friends, but both Annette and Sandy couldn't help feeling disappointed to find that there were no young people among the guests.

As soon as they had finished lunch, Annette managed to pull Sandy aside for a moment. She nodded toward the calm sweep of ocean visible through the trees that lined the terrace. "Is that water out there good for swimming?" she asked.

Sandy grinned. "Let's find out the hard way." And they excused themselves politely and disappeared into the house as quickly as possible. While the lively chatter continued on the terrace, they slipped down to the private beach and stretched out on the warm sand.

They had fun swimming out to the anchored raft and back, between sunning sessions, and Sandy almost forgot for a while that she didn't like San Benito.

Once, Annette saw a tall young man a short distance up the beach. He seemed to be watching them, but she couldn't quite make out what he looked like because the sun was in her eyes. And when she looked that way a minute later, he had disappeared among the shoreline rocks.

She decided not to say anything about it to

Sandy. Sandy would surely think he was a dangerous character!

When the breeze came up late in the afternoon, it brought a chill with it, and they decided to go back to the house.

"Maybe we should take a riding lesson and warm up," Annette suggested. "There's still plenty of sunshine left."

"I'm too tired," Sandy said, yawning. "Remember, I was awake half the night. Let's start out early in the morning."

There was no one in sight at the stables the next morning when they arrived dressed in some old riding gear. Annette insisted that Sandy wear riding boots during these practice rides, so she could get used to the feel of them while she was trying to learn to stay in the saddle.

Annette still had many misgivings about the wisdom of Sandy's trying to become an expert in a short time. She hoped fervently nothing would happen. She would feel guilty if Sandy got dumped off again.

They heard a horse in one of the farthest stalls kicking restlessly. "Bet that's Black Prince," Annette said excitedly. "Let's go have a quick look at him as long as there's nobody around to warn us off."

"Not me!" Sandy said promptly. "He probably has long horns and a forked tail, and he'll break down the stall door to trample us!"

But Annette took a firm hold of her arm and dragged her along, protesting. There were stalls for twenty horses, but only eight or ten were in use. Then came empty ones, and far down at the end was a stall with the name BLACK PRINCE above it.

As the girls moved along, peering into each stall, an occasional gray or brown head came out to stare inquisitively at the visitors and nicker a greeting.

Annette simply had to stop and pet each one as she went by, but Sandy kept a couple of feet clear of the open stalls. Someday she might love horses the way Annette did, but it would take time.

"I think I'll go look for Patrick," Sandy said

nervously as Annette finally came to the stall with Black Prince's name above it, and a jet-black snorting head was thrust out suddenly toward her.

The head was huge and the horse it belonged to was very tall. Even Annette was startled into taking a step backward.

"Now, now, boy! Don't scare the ladies!" A small, wiry old man was hurrying in, leading two mild-looking young mares who were already saddled and bridled. His voice was soft with a brogue, and at the soothing sound of it the big black horse seemed to relax. Now he was taking some inquiring sniffs in the direction of Annette, but there was nothing threatening about him.

"He's gorgeous!" Annette said breathlessly. "You angel, you!" She held out a hand for him to sniff as she spoke. "Golly! I'd love to have one just like you someday!"

Black Prince threw his head back and neighed. It was almost as if he had understood her words. When he lowered his head again, he nuzzled her hand gently, as if coaxing to be petted.

The old groom left the two mares tied a few feet away and came up, chuckling. "Go ahead and pet the big baby, miss. He's gentle as a lamb if he knows you like him."

Annette stroked the big horse's soft nose, and he whinnied softly in response. But Sandy kept a safe distance away. "Mrs. Glaven says he's dangerous. Better look out, Annette."

The old groom snorted. "It's for her own reasons she says that," he said angrily, "and to devil her stepson, young Master Brod."

"Oh, I haven't met him. How old is he?" Sandy asked.

"About your age or a mite more. But he don't live here no longer, miss."

"Does Black Prince belong to him?" Annette asked, patting the big stallion affectionately on his forehead.

"Did belong, miss," Patrick said with a growl, "but not anymore. 'Tis herself owns him now, worse luck for the poor lad." He scowled off at the house as he spoke.

Annette started to ask him to explain, but

before she could, Patrick said hastily, "I'm sorry. I talk too much, little ladies. I'd take it kindly if you wouldn't tell the madam I mentioned the lad." He seemed worried.

"Of course we won't, Patrick," Sandy assured him.

"It might mean my job and Mary's if she knew," he said sadly, "and we've been in service here a long time."

"Please, don't worry," Annette told him gravely, "we won't say a word."

As they rode off a few minutes later toward the rear of the property, Annette asked Sandy, "Is Patrick married to the upstairs maid who talked to you? Is that the Mary he means?"

Sandy nodded. "They're both old-timers left over from the days of Mr. Glaven's first wife."

"I wonder where 'Master Brod' is, and why Patrick feels so sorry for him?" Annette mused as they rode together around the practice ring.

"I think I'll ask some questions," Sandy said with a grin.

"I wouldn't," Annette replied quickly. "You might stir up something, and after all, it doesn't seem to be any of our business."

And Sandy, rather reluctantly, had to agree.

7 *The Old Adobe*

Annette and Sandy managed to get in quite a bit of riding practice during the next couple of days, almost all of it along the private beach. They jumped over logs, raced through the surf, and in many ways became used to pretty rugged riding. Sandy was getting quite sure of herself, but Annette still had qualms about her joining in the hunt.

It was a cloudy morning with a threat of rain when the two started out in Annette's Monster to pick up their boots and have one last fitting of their new riding habits.

"Hope it doesn't rain on the big day so they have to call off the hunt!" Sandy scowled at the dark sky.

"No such luck!" Annette said, and she meant it. "They'd ride if it snowed and hailed!"

"Suits me!" Sandy declared recklessly. "And

by the way, what was it Mrs. Glaven told you about Black Prince just as we left? I missed it," Sandy said as they sped toward the center of San Benito through the older part of the town.

"She said we wouldn't have to worry about keeping clear of 'that horrible creature' much longer, because she has sent word to some man named Murray, who has a horse ranch up near Salinas, to come and buy him. It seems he's been after the horse for ages."

"I'm sort of glad. I don't trust him nearly as much as you do. I'm sure he'd bite one of us if he had half a chance, no matter what old Patrick says."

"Pooh!" Annette said. And something else under the hood said, *"Sput! Sput—spu-u-ut!"* and the Monster started to slow down.

"Oops! Out of gas?" Sandy guessed as Annette pulled at the choke without much effect. "There's an old beat-up station just ahead. Can we make it?"

"Just about, I think!" Annette said, coaxing the expiring engine with the last few drops of gasoline that were in the tank.

They limped into the small station and looked for someone to come to the rescue. But no one was around.

Annette could hear the sound of a heavy car motor running inside a small shedlike building that must have been part of a carriage house years before. Someone was working on a car.

She signaled with her horn, but the unseen mechanic failed to come out and the motor in the shed kept on alternately roaring and then sputtering out.

She swung out of the car and marched over to poke her head in through the doorway. A figure in coveralls grimy with grease was bending over the motor of a black sports car. He was whistling as he worked on something inside the hood.

Annette went up to him and pulled at his sleeve.

He straightened up quickly and turned to face her. She saw that he was tall and slim and had a shock of sandy hair that stood up every which way on his head. His face was smudged on both cheeks, and there was a streak of black grease on the tip of his nose.

Annette couldn't help smiling at the picture he made, and he saw it. He reached quickly for a cap hanging on a hook on the wall and pulled it on over the unruly hair.

"Sorry, I didn't hear you pull in," he said, reaching hastily to turn off the motor. "Gas?"

But Annette was staring at the odd-looking, red-and-white cap. She knew she had seen one like it lately, but for the moment she couldn't remember where. She nodded.

He glanced out the doorway. "Your car?" he asked admiringly. "Nice buggy. But I like my own homemade bomb!" He patted the hood of the black sports car affectionately. "There's nothing like the one you build yourself!" Then he went on out.

Annette studied the black car a moment. Black sports car, red-and-white cap, tall young man—it added up. She knew where she had seen the combination before.

It had been several days ago at the entrance to

the Glaven estate. This was the car and the tall young fellow who had almost run into the Monster the afternoon she arrived!

And that meant he was the one who had quarreled with Mrs. Glaven over something about money.

On an impulse, she leaned over and studied the name on the registration card while the young man headed out to fill up the Monster. The registered owner was Broderick Glaven, and the address was 567 Mill Road, wherever that might be. Master Brod, in person! she said to herself. What do you know? And she hurried out to take another look.

She didn't mention her discovery until she and Sandy were well on their way again to the tailor shop.

"Brod Glaven? Are you sure? What on earth would he be doing in an old run-down place like that?" Sandy's blue eyes were saucer-round.

"Working for a living, I suppose. People do, sometimes," Annette teased. She had noticed Sandy's eyes following Brod around while he was filling the Monster's tank and testing the tires. She knew Sandy had been quite interested.

"Oh, darn!" Sandy slid down in her seat and pouted. "I was hoping that—oh, I guess it's just as well. Dad and I won't be around here long enough for me to get to know him very well, anyhow."

They were on their way home before Sandy mentioned him again. They had both been wondering just what the trouble was between him and his stepmother. "Maybe if we could find out why he and Mrs. Glaven were arguing, we could help fix it up," she said. But Annette had no ideas how to start finding out, except by questioning the servants, and they had agreed not to do that.

After lunch they rode out together to try a nearby hill trail for the first time. It was a "natural" one that was seldom used. It was supposed to lead past the original Glaven home, which was built of adobe bricks made by Native Americans who had lived in this area before the state was established, over a hundred years ago. Mrs. Glaven had been vague about how much of the adobe was still standing.

The two girls rode to where a faint trace of the old trail remained. It wound up and around a hill. Annette studied it. "It doesn't look so tricky from here. I imagine stray cattle use it. But if there's a heavy rain, it might wash out and leave us stranded on top of a mountain or something."

But Sandy was game to try it, so they began the climb. It wasn't bad at the start. There were beautiful wildflowers covering the slopes above and beyond them, and a tiny stream meandered along through thickets of toyon on the canyon's floor below the trail.

Then the trail became overgrown with tall brush that had to be thrust aside for passage. Sandy groaned exasperatedly as a branch snatched the scarf off her head.

"Let me go ahead and see if it gets worse. No use in both of us fighting through this stuff," Annette said. "You wait here."

But she had gone only a few feet when a big flash of lightning was followed by a crash of thunder. Sandy's mare took off like a shot with Sandy hanging on desperately, too frightened to do anything but scream.

Annette and her horse were almost knocked off the trail and into a ditch, but she managed to control the animal and guide it hastily after the runaway.

On they went, with Sandy's horse almost flying and Annette trying valiantly to catch up.

Now it was raining. Not just a pup-and-kitten downpour, but a full-fledged cats-and-dogs cloudburst.

The horses slipped and slid on the trail, and gradually Sandy's horse began to slow down. The moment it did, Annette closed the gap between them and soon had the runaway's bridle in a firm grip. And in a few yards more, Sandy's horse decided it had had enough fun for one day and came peacefully to a stop in a grassy clearing at the edge of the woods.

For the last quarter mile, Sandy had been riding with her eyes closed, bent as flat as she could get on the saddle. Now, as she realized that her horse had come to a stop, she straightened up, opened her eyes, and looked at Annette, who still had hold of the bridle. "I stayed on this time!" she told Annette triumphantly. "I guess I'm learning to ride!"

Annette was so weak from the strain she had just been through that she was almost falling out of the saddle herself. But Sandy's remark struck her so funny that she started to laugh, and Sandy soon joined her in somewhat hysterical shouts of laughter.

When they recovered a little, they took a look around through the sheets of rain and discovered that they were very close to a two-story adobe house.

It stood there, lonely and apparently deserted, between two tall, skinny palm trees that rose bare-trunked for forty or fifty feet straight into the air and then were capped by dripping crowns of fronds. The fronds hung limp, for all the world like damp feather dusters.

"The original adobe, I suppose," Sandy said. "I thought it was almost in ruins, but that looks as if it still has a mighty tight roof. Let's try to get in out of this stuff that they call a heavy mist around here."

They ran for the heavy wooden door, pulling the resisting horses along behind them.

A few feet from the door an ancient wooden rail stretched between two heavy, hand-hewn posts. It was the hitch rail where old-time visitors tied their horses while they went inside and paid their compliments to the original Glavens. The girls looped their reins over the rail and tied them securely. Their saddles were already as wet as they could possibly get, so there was no use taking them off the horses.

Sandy walked stiffly to the big door and pulled hard on the iron knocker. A sound reverberated through the empty house, but no one came to open the door.

"I guess the Glaven ghosts don't have any manners!" Annette laughed. "They could at least say, 'Come in for a while and dry off.'"

Sandy shivered and gave the door a push.

To their amazement, it creaked open on rusty

iron hinges. It didn't go far on the warped, heavy wooden floor, but they could see inside by the faint light coming from high, narrow windows with deep sills. The big downstairs room was empty, but there was no debris of old relics, or cobwebs to tangle in their hair. It seemed as if it had just been swept.

"It looks pretty neat. I'll say that much for the Glaven ghosts," Annette remarked as she and Sandy stepped inside.

The walls were whitewashed adobe bricks, and the big fireplace, in which a man could stand upright, was blackened by countless fires. But there was a neat pile of firewood at one side of it, as if someone expected to light it into leaping life on just such a rainy day.

The only catch to it was that neither girl had any matches. They could only shiver in their wet clothes.

"If we only had s-something to wrap up in," Sandy said, through chattering teeth.

Annette looked up at the gallery that went across the entire back of the main room. There were two closed doors up there. "Maybe we could find some old drapes or something up there to wrap around us while our blouses dry a little," she suggested. "Come on."

Sandy wasn't too keen about the idea of going into those rooms. "They're probably full of spiders or m-mice," she said, protesting unhappily.

"There weren't any down here, were there?" Annette argued good-naturedly. "Let's arm ourselves and brave the enemy!" She took up a slender length of firewood and put it over her shoulder as if it were a rifle. "Forward march!"

Sandy smiled and then grabbed another piece of wood, and they went up the narrow stairway side by side, testing each step carefully but finding them all strong and reliable.

They pushed open the first door at the head of the stairs and stood staring in amazement at what was in the room beyond it.

8 *An Angry Young Man*

A faint, rain-dimmed light shone into the white-washed room from a window high on the wall. It revealed several piles of leather-bound books of different sizes, and boxes of papers covered with handwriting and typing. Most of the papers were in folders that looked as if they had been used in a filing case.

Nearby, a large box was filled with silver cups; large silver plates engraved with names and dates; blue, red, and white trophy ribbons tucked in around them; and a silver statue of a horse. There were boots leaning against the box and a silver-mounted riding crop lying across their tops.

But there was no dust on any of it.

"Looks like somebody's moving in!" Sandy commented as they crossed the threshold. She started over to examine some of the trophies in the box, but before she could take more than a few steps, they both heard a car motor approaching. "A car!" Sandy could hardly believe it.

"Uh-oh," Annette said quickly, "there must be a road coming in the other way. We'd better get out of here fast in case the car stops."

She had no sooner spoken than the motor died. The car had stopped. And whoever was in it must have seen their two horses tied to the hitch rail. There wasn't a chance of getting away without being seen.

"I guess we're in for a bawling out for trespassing." Sandy made a face. "It's probably the new tenant, whoever it is."

"Let's go down and find out. We might as well get it over with," Annette said glumly.

But before they had even reached the door, there were quick steps below, then on the stairway. "Hey! Who's up there? What do you think you're doing?" The masculine voice was threatening and they stopped and hung on to each other for mutual support.

"He sounds angry," Sandy whispered. "Golly!"

Then they saw who it was. Brod Glaven, fists doubled threateningly, stepped in through the doorway. But almost at once he recognized them and relaxed. "Hey, what are you two doing here?"

"It was r-raining," Sandy said, shivering, "and we got soaked. We didn't mean to snoop, Brod, honestly. We didn't know anybody was moving in here."

"I'm not moving in," Brod said hurriedly. Then he stopped, frowning. "How do you know who I am?"

Annette told him with a saucy grin, "Read it on your car registration card this morning."

"Oh." He smiled slightly. "I see." Then he looked puzzled. "But how did you get way out here, and on horseback?"

It was Sandy's turn. "We're staying at your stepmother's."

Brod scowled. "And I suppose she discovered I was moving these things out here, and she sent you to look them over."

"Not at all," Annette said quickly. "Sandy just

explained to you how we happened to come here."

"That's right!" Sandy's eyes flashed. "It's true. Besides, we don't have to take orders from Mrs. Glaven. We just happen to be staying there because she's trying her level best to unload that crummy old house and the rest of her property on my father!"

Brod Glaven look startled, and then his face relaxed into a friendly grin. "The Burnetts. I've heard."

"Dad hasn't fallen for it yet, and he won't if I have anything to say about it!" Sandy assured him defiantly.

"Suits me!" Brod said grimly. "Besides, you might not have it very long if—" He broke off abruptly and refused to explain just what he meant. All he would say was, "Why don't you ask my stepmother? She owns the place."

Annette was still puzzling over what he had said earlier. "Why did you think Mrs. Glaven had sent us to look at all this stuff?" And she guessed, "It's hers, isn't it?"

Brod looked sober. "Not now. You see, it was in my father's study when he passed away two years ago. She dumped it into a storage warehouse and had the room redecorated as a sitting room for herself. It was only a few days ago that I found out where his books and trophies were."

"How did you find out?" Sandy asked eagerly.

"A man who works at the warehouse told me he'd been cataloging some things that were to be sold by the company for nonpayment of charges, and he had seen those trophies in the lot. So I dug up the cash and bailed all of it out." He picked up one of the silver cups and studied it most affectionately before he laid it down.

"Did your father win all these cups and things?" Sandy was awed. She picked up a silver plate and read the inscription, wide-eyed.

"Most of them, but a couple are *mine* and Black Prince's," Brod explained proudly. "Here's a photo of us winning the Jumper Sweepstakes five years ago when I was a kid." He showed them the framed print proudly. "He's the greatest!"

"How is it that your stepmother owns him now?" Annette asked.

Brod frowned. "She got legal title to all the horses as part of my father's estate."

"That's so unjust!" Sandy exclaimed indignantly.

Brod shrugged. "I tried to buy Black Prince from her a couple of days ago, but she wouldn't make a deal. She claims she's going to have him gentled and ride him herself at the next show." He scowled. "She'll ruin him!"

The girls looked quickly at each other. That must have been the row that Sandy had partly overheard.

Suddenly, Annette remembered something. "She must have changed her mind. She was just telling us that tomorrow she's going to sell Black Prince to some man who runs a horse farm somewhere."

"Oh, no! She can't do that! I won't let her! I'll—I'll—" He couldn't find a word for a moment. "I'll stop her somehow!" His face was twisted with anger.

"How can you do that? You said she legally owns him." Annette spoke calmly, and it seemed to quiet him.

"Yeah, I forgot for a minute," he said slowly. "I guess there's not much I can do about it."

But Annette noticed that he still wore the angry look, and she thought, I can tell he hasn't given up yet. I hope he doesn't do anything rash!

Sandy sneezed a couple of times just then, and Brod seemed to notice for the first time that they were soaking wet.

"Gosh!" he exclaimed. "I'm sorry! I let you stand here, shivering, when there's plenty of wood downstairs and a fireplace to pile it into. Come on and dry out!"

And he hurried them along downstairs.

A few minutes later, they were drying out before a roaring fire while the thunderstorm outside gradually died away in the distance and the sun came out.

Brod was in the midst of trying to explain to Sandy some highly technical details about building a car engine when Annette, who had

practically no interest in the subject, said, "Hey, Sandy! How about that riding lesson we're supposed to be taking?"

"Oh, there's no hurry, is there?" Sandy looked appealingly at her friend. But Annette got up off the floor where they were sitting and insisted that they had better go before it got too late.

"I'll be going, too," Brod said after a quick glance at his watch. "I'm on the late shift tonight, two to ten. But I've got to bring in my last load of books first. I've been dashing between here and the warehouse all day."

"We wondered why the door was left unlocked," Sandy told him.

"Well, it will be locked this time," he said with a grin. He drew a big iron key out of his coat pocket. "This big fellow is a hundred years old and still does a pretty good job of keeping intruders out. I'm the only person who has a key to the place," he boasted slightly.

It took him only a minute or two to get the books from his car and take them up to the gallery room. While he was gone, the girls smothered the last embers of the fire.

Then they all left together. As he closed the door and locked it behind them, Annette asked, "What about people getting in through the windows?"

"Anybody wider than ten inches couldn't get in. Those openings were really not windows, just airholes. And besides, nobody knows I'm storing Dad's things here and nobody needs to know. As for his papers, after I finish checking them over and looking through his books for something, I'll donate them to the historical society. They've been in the family for generations."

Annette thought, I wonder what he thinks he'll find in those old books. Family history, maybe.

He helped them mount and watched them ride off. Sandy turned in her saddle to wave to him as they approached the first turn in the trail, but he had disappeared, and a moment later they heard the distant roar of his car motor.

"Boy!" Sandy grinned. "Was he ever angry about his horse being sold! I thought he was going to rush right out and do something about it!" She sobered suddenly. "I wish—I wish I could help him!"

Annette nodded. "He doesn't seem to be getting a very good deal, but there's nothing you could do to stop Mrs. Glaven from selling Black Prince. I think she's doing it for spite."

They rode in silence a little while and then Annette said suddenly, "Hey, how much do you want to help Brod? Could you do a little acting?"

"Acting? Why, whatever has that to do with his horse?" Sandy asked, wide-eyed.

"If you could manage to be there tomorrow when the man from the horse farm comes to buy Black Prince, you could make believe you want the horse for yourself!"

"But I'm scared of him!" Sandy shuddered.

"That's where your acting comes in," Annette explained. "If you can convince your father that you've simply got to own Black Prince, I'm sure he'll top any bid that the farm man makes. And *she* won't be able to refuse it."

"Oh, Annette, that's a wonderful idea! But you've got to be there, too, and help me!"

They discussed it eagerly as they rode on, and Sandy was so happy over the prospect of helping Brod that she willingly worked at learning how to ride and even endeavored one jump, which turned out well.

"And when Black Prince is mine, Brod can ride him whenever he wants to!" Sandy said out loud.

Annette wondered what had become of Sandy's fierce resolution not to let her father buy the Glaven estate. She seemed to have forgotten it. Annette decided not to remind her. Sandy might be happier in San Benito, after all.

Late that night, after Sandy had fallen asleep, Annette sat by the window in her own room, writing a letter to Aunt Lila.

—So, maybe I can soon be on my way home. It's lovely here, of course, and right now the tide is out and the moonlight is making a shining path across the little harbor waves. It's all so still. I

guess I must be the only one awake around here-

Annette paused to look out the window again at the moonlight and promptly dropped her pen in surprise. Something was moving across the lawn not fifty feet away.

It was a man. There was something familiar about his tall figure and the swing of his arms as he strode in the direction of the stables. Then she spotted the cap on the back of his head. Suddenly, she knew who it was—Brod!

But what was Brod Glaven doing here in the middle of the night?

Almost at once she thought she had guessed the answer. He was coming to steal Black Prince so Mrs. Glaven couldn't sell the horse!

Oh, he mustn't try to do that! she thought excitedly. He'll spoil our plan to help him! I've got to catch him!

And a moment later she went rushing out of the room, down the stairs, and out the front door toward the stables.

9 *Brod's Story*

Annette raced across the moonlit lawn toward the Glaven stable. There was no sign of Brod, but she felt sure that he had been heading there.

Then, as she came around the corner of the long, low building that housed the horses, she caught sight of him. He was unlatching the Dutch door of Black Prince's stall.

That seemed to mean that she had guessed right, and he intended to steal the big stallion that had been his pride and joy. And she knew that she had to stop him before he spoiled everything that she and Sandy had schemed to do to help him.

He was going inside the stall now, and she was almost at the beginning of the long row of stalls. She didn't want to risk arousing one of the sleeping stable hands, so she hurried on silently, though she was tempted to call softly to Brod.

She could hear Black Prince whickering and knew that he and Brod were having a joyful reunion.

Then, at the other end of the row of stalls, she saw the reflection of a flashlight and heard hurried footsteps approaching. She stopped at once and darted into the shadow of the overhanging roof, flattening herself against the wall in the hope that whoever it was wouldn't glance her way.

But with the bright beam getting closer and the footsteps louder, she realized she would have to find a better place in which to hide. She managed to reach the nearest of the empty stalls and disappear into it just as the light swept along the wooden walk.

She heard Brod's voice call softly, "Is that you, Pat?"

"No, it ain't, Mister whoever-you-are! What do you think you're doin' in there?"

Annette recognized the voice of the new stableman who had taken her horse and Sandy's earlier that afternoon when they had come back from their ride.

"Minding my own business!" Brod's voice came angrily through the dark.

Annette peeked out and saw Brod stride out of the big stallion's stall and start past the stableman. But the man clubbed Brod with his flashlight, and Brod grabbed his wrist as they struggled. The stable man tripped and went down hard on his back. He carried Brod down with him, but Brod was on his feet instantly and backing off. The stable man sat up, rubbing his head, yelling, "Help! Robbers! Help!"

Brod stood a moment, uncertainly. He didn't seem to know what to do. Annette could hear shouts and the sounds of men running. In another moment, they would be swarming all over the place.

Annette stepped out. "Brod!" she hissed. And when he looked over, bewildered, she beckoned him to come to her. "Quick!" she said in a husky stage whisper. The running feet were almost there.

Brod ran toward her. The stable man continued to yell, but made no effort to get to his feet.

Annette grabbed Brod and drew him into the empty stall with her a second before the chauffeur, a robe hastily thrown over his night-clothes, ran in, followed by the old head groom, Patrick, and another stable man.

She and Brod crouched there in the darkness while the excited stable man told about surprising the intruder who had gotten away, probably down the driveway or into the woods.

There was a great deal of confusion, and everyone seemed to be trying to talk at once. Brod heard his own name mentioned by the other stable man, but at once old Patrick snorted, "Master Brod? Nonsense, Bill! More likely it was Tim O'Neill—it was him that used to take care of Prince."

And after another small chorus of voices, Patrick's voice came again. "There's no use in gettin' the Madam upset. Tim meant no harm, I'm sure. He was fond of Prince, and I been lettin' him come now an' then to say hello an' give the animal a wee lump of sugar."

The voices went away, but Annette and Brod stayed cramped in the stall for a few minutes longer, waiting.

Annette became aware suddenly that Brod was quietly laughing. She asked, startled, "What's so funny?"

"Tim O'Neill went to Ireland last month, but Patrick's the only one who knows that," he said with a chuckle. "Good old Pat!"

"You mean he's deliberately misleading them because he knows you're the one who was trying to steal Black Prince?" Annette was surprised.

"Just a minute, sis!" Brod got to his feet quickly, scowling. "I wasn't trying to steal him. I only came to say good-bye because you said she was selling him tomorrow!"

"Oh!" Annette was relieved. "My mistake!"

"I have to admit I *did* think of trying to steal him, but where does a guy who lives in a one-room apartment hide a horse?" he asked, with a shrug of his shoulders. "Besides, she'd be sure to suspect me."

"Mrs. Glaven?" Annette asked, but she knew without his answer.

He nodded glumly. "Sure." He turned to her suddenly. "Thanks for rescuing me, but how did you happen to be wandering around out here this time of night?"

Annette explained about seeing him cross the lawn. "And I wanted to tell you not to do anything rash because Sandy's going to get her father to buy Black Prince for her tomorrow. Then you can ride your horse whenever you want to."

"Does she really mean that?" Brod demanded happily. And when Annette nodded, he said soberly, "That girl's a real-live doll!"

"I'll tell her you said so," Annette promised pertly.

It was very quiet outside now, and Brod poked his head out briefly. "All clear," he told Annette. And a minute later, they were hurrying away from the stable.

At any second, Annette expected to hear shouts and a hullabaloo behind them, but nothing happened. They reached the front of the house safely and stopped by the hedge.

"Where did you leave your car?" Annette whispered.

"Two houses down," he told her. "Nobody will hear me start it that far away."

"Good!" Annette nodded. "I'd better say good night now and dash." She took a step away, with a wave of her hand.

"Wait, please. You said that if the Burnetts buy Black Prince, I can ride him when I want to. Does that mean they have decided to buy this place?"

"It's beginning to look that way," Annette said, laughing softly, "in spite of warning messages."

"The note, you mean," Brod said soberly.

Annette was surprised. "Oh, you've heard about that."

Brod nodded a little sheepishly. "I wrote it, and a good friend of mine put it under one of the Burnetts' doors."

Annette knew it must have been Mary, but she didn't tell him that she had guessed. Instead, she asked curiously, "How would it help you to scare away people who might want to buy the estate?"

"It would help make things a lot simpler later on," he said soberly. "You see, one of these days, if I have any luck, I expect to prove to everybody that Mrs. Glaven doesn't have the legal rights to sell it, because half of it is mine!"

"But you said yourself she inherited it legally."

"She did, by the terms of the will my father's lawyers filed. But I know he made another will after that one, though I haven't been able to find any trace of it yet."

"Wouldn't his lawyers know about it?" Annette asked.

"Not if it was a holographic will, and I'm sure it was."

"Whatever kind that is!" Annette looked puzzled.

"It's a handwritten will, signed and dated by the person who writes it. It doesn't have to be in legal language, just as long as the meaning is clear."

"Oh," Annette said quickly, "then that's what you're going to look for in those books and papers at the adobe?"

Brod nodded soberly. "It's just about my last chance for finding it. Mrs. Glaven has forbidden me to come into the house again. She says my father never promised me he'd change his will; that it's all a lie to make trouble for her and spoil the sale of the house."

"But why did your dad leave you out of that other will?" Annette asked.

"Dad and I had a row. It was a humdinger. We have the same kind of tempers. I mean, we *had*. Poor Dad. He wanted me to go to Europe with them when I finished high school, but I refused. I wanted to work out some ideas I had about building my car. So I stayed home and they went alone. He was so angry that he wouldn't let me come down to see them off at the train."

"That is too bad," Annette agreed. "But I guess he got over it, didn't he?"

"Oh, sure. When they got back, he and I forgot the whole thing except when *she* would give me a dig about it. Dad and I went hunting one day and he told me he was changing his will back again, dividing everything between my stepmother and me. He said he'd tend to it the next day."

"Why didn't he tell her?"

"He did," Brod said grimly. "The whole staff heard the row that night. It went on for a couple of hours in his study, with her yelling and threatening to leave if he changed the will again. He was sick the next day, very sick. Heart problems, the doctors said. And he didn't get well. She claimed it was the hunting trip that brought it on, but I know it was the quarrel," he said bitterly.

A distant church bell tolled twice, and Brod told Annette abruptly, "You'd better run on in. I'm sorry I got wound up, feeling sorry for myself. Please tell Sandy I think she's a darling about Black Prince. And thanks!"

A moment later he was striding off. Annette hoped she could remember all the things he had told her so she could tell Sandy everything in the morning.

She hurried upstairs, half tempted to go knock on Sandy's door right then and tell her. But she decided that Sandy was too tired to be disturbed, so she stopped at her own door.

She was surprised to find it standing open a few inches. She felt certain that she had closed it when she had hurried out. Someone must have been here. Someone who might be waiting in her room. For a moment she felt a little shiver of fear. Then she remembered that the note hadn't been a threat, after all. I'm getting as spooked as Sandy, she told herself. And before she could give in to a temptation to turn and run, she pushed the door open all the way and stared into the dark room as boldly as she could.

10   *A Lovely Gift*

Annette could hardly believe her eyes. The figure facing her in the light from the hallway was Sandy! There she was, glaring angrily at her and saying reproachfully, "I hope you two had a lovely time, sneaking out while I was sound asleep!"

"Sandy! What on earth—?"

"Oh, don't make believe! I saw you and Brod standing down there talking—" Her voice broke. "And after you knew how much I liked him and wanted to help him! Ohhh!" It was a wail of fury and grief. "I wish I'd never met either of you!" She collapsed into the nearest satin-cushioned chair and wept.

Annette's patience was strained for a moment. Then her sense of humor took over. "Oh, Sandy! And just when I had such exciting things to tell you! But there's no use now. You wouldn't be interested!" She made it sound quite casual as she went over and switched on a lamp.

There were a couple of large sniffs from Sandy, but Annette pretended not to notice and kicked off her shoes and yawned loudly. Then Sandy's voice came hesitantly. "Exciting things?"

"Mm-hmm," Annette agreed, busily pulling off her socks. "Like, he thinks you're a doll for planning to buy Black Prince."

"He does?" Sandy had forgotten her tears. "Go on!"

"Oh, lots more. Like why his stepmother inherited this place."

"Please, Annette, I'm sorry I was jealous. Tell me everything he told you!"

So Annette did, down to the smallest details, and it was almost dawn before they had finished plotting what they could do to help Brod Glaven.

"First," Annette said sleepily, "there's that horse dealer coming in the morning. Do you still think you can get your dad to outbid him for Black Prince?"

"Nothing's going to stop me," Sandy said, and Annette knew from the way she said it that Jim Burnett would have his hands full if he opposed his daughter.

Sandy began her campaign at breakfast before the horse rancher arrived. There never, she told her father, had been such a wonderful horse as Black Prince. She had actually fallen in love with him the moment she had seen him, and now she simply had to have him.

"But Mrs. Glaven says he's vicious, honey. I don't want you taking any chances. A good steady mare would be better. Maybe today I can pick one up from Murray that would suit you." Her father beamed at her.

Annette, discreetly keeping out of the conversation, noticed that Mr. Burnett seemed happy that his daughter showed an interest in anything around the Glaven estate, especially after her antagonism toward buying it. She nodded encouragingly at Sandy and kicked her gently under the table.

Sandy took the hint. "Black Prince is the one I want, Dad. But maybe we'd just better forget all about buying any horses since I don't want to live in San Benito, anyhow."

Annette saw that Mr. Burnett looked worried. Then Sandy added the finishing touch. She sighed audibly and said, "Of course, if I owned Black Prince, I might feel differently. I could win cups and have my picture in the paper. Or, if he's too hard for me to manage, *you* could ride him in the horse show!"

Jim Burnett's eyes gleamed. Annette could see that he liked the idea a lot. All he needed was a gentle shove.

So, she said innocently, "Sandy, that's a super idea! I hear that Black Prince is the best jumper in the county. I'm sure your dad would win a lot of ribbons with him."

"Sure, why not?" Jim Burnett's big laugh rang through the dining room as Mrs. Glaven came in. "It's a deal, Sandy girl!"

"What *is* going on?" Mrs. Glaven asked brightly.

"You can tell that horse feller Murray that Black Prince isn't for sale! I'm buying that horse for Sandy and me. I'll top whatever he offers."

Annette noticed that their hostess didn't seem very happy over this statement. "I don't know if you should take a chance with Black Prince," Mrs. Glaven said with a frown. "He's dangerous. And besides, my stepson may make trouble if Black Prince remains around here. I'm convinced that he's the one who tried to steal the horse last night."

Annette and Sandy exchanged quick, worried looks.

"I hope you notified the police!" Mr. Burnett said grimly.

"I did. But Higgins, the new stableman who stopped him, couldn't positively identify Brod because he had never seen him before, so they would do nothing."

"Master Brod's no thief, ma'am! If it was him, and I doubt it, he surely didn't come to steal!" It was Mary, glaring defiantly at her mistress from the kitchen door. She was bringing in fresh coffee on a silver tray. "I'll take me oath on that!"

"That will do, Mary!" Mrs. Glaven's voice was sharp. "You may put down that tray and go."

"Yes, ma'am!" Mary put her tray down with a bang on the lace-covered table and turned to march out of the room, head held high. The door swung violently after her, but no one spoke until it finally came to a stop.

Mrs. Glaven broke the silence. She was so angry, Annette noticed, that her knuckles were white as she gripped the edge of the table. "I do my best for them, and all I get in return is ingratitude! They're all against me, and it's my stepson's fault—every bit of it. He's turned them all with his silly lies!" She burst into tears and got up quickly, dabbing at her eyes with her handkerchief.

Jim Burnett rose and hurried around the table to her. "Now, now, please don't talk like that! We're your friends, and if there's anything we can do," he told her, "all you have to do is let us know! Please don't let it get you down."

"Oh, thank you!" She lifted her face with a wan little smile. "I'm sorry I'm such a helpless creature!" She blinked at him. "You're so terribly thoughtful, Mr. Burnett!"

Oh, brother! Annette thought. The clinging-vine act! And she almost giggled out loud as Peggy Glaven moved toward the terrace door, clinging to Jim Burnett's arm. The girls heard her say, "Nobody understands—" as she and big Jim went out into the sunshine.

"Something tells me she's about to add another ten thousand to the price of this place," Sandy said wryly. "And Dad will be soft enough to let the poor, helpless little thing get away with it."

"Only maybe she won't be the owner by the time the final papers are ready to sign. Maybe Brod will own half," Annette suggested. "We've simply got to help him find that missing will!"

As Annette finished speaking, they both were startled by a sound from the direction of the kitchen door. It was Mary again, and she was beaming at them as she tiptoed in.

"Bless your dear hearts! It's good to know

Master Brod has friends in this house. But Patrick and I have looked high and low for that paper you're talkin' about, and it's not to be found." Mary sighed gloomily. "It's my thought that herself has already found it and it's gone up in smoke!"

"Oh, I hope not!" Sandy moaned.

"Of course, if she has found it, she still might have it hidden somewhere," Annette reasoned. "Where haven't you looked around the house, Mary?"

"Not many places, Miss Annette. Herself's room, for one. There's a desk drawer I've pulled at many a time, but it's always locked."

"You should wear hairpins," Annette joked. "I've heard they're great for opening locks!"

"I tried that, too, but I haven't the knack!" Mary admitted with a giggle.

Sandy didn't say anything, but she had a strange look on her pretty face. It wasn't until a couple of hours later that Annette found out what that strange look meant.

Annette was putting on her slacks and sweater,

set to go for a ride out to the adobe house with Sandy. I hope Brod has found something in those books and papers from his father's study, she thought. And I wonder where Sandy has been the last hour. She disappeared right after lunch.

She had barely finished the thought when her door flew open with a bang, and Sandy rushed in and closed the door behind her hastily. Her face was flushed with excitement, and her eyes were like round blue saucers.

"Whatever's the matter now?" Annette stared at her.

Sandy sank down on the edge of Annette's bed and held up an object she had been carrying in her hand. Annette was startled to see that it was a big, old-fashioned wire hairpin. "I nearly got caught! She came in while I was trying to open that nasty old desk drawer, and I had to hide behind a screen!"

"Oh, Sandy! Why did you pull such a silly trick? Are you sure she didn't see you?" Annette was really shocked.

"I wouldn't be here now if she had! She'd

have snatched me bald-headed!" Sandy shook her head. "Whew! Is she ever in a terrible bind!"

"What do you mean?" Annette frowned.

"I mean she's having bill trouble, but good! She phoned some decorator company and practically begged them not to sue her for what she owes them for refurnishing this house. And she's promised to pay them five thousand dollars tomorrow morning—in cash!"

"Five thousand in cash!" Annette repeated, amazed.

"I wonder where she thinks she's going to get it." Sandy knitted her brows.

"Maybe your father has decided to go ahead and buy the place from her, and he's giving her a down payment of five thousand dollars," Annette guessed.

Sandy shook her head quickly. "I saw him half an hour ago and asked him not to do anything about buying it for a little while. And he promised he wouldn't."

Annette was thoughtful. "You know," she said after a moment, "I feel sort of sorry for Mrs.

Glaven. I don't think she's mean or anything. I think she's just plain dizzy. She doesn't know how to handle money and gets all mixed up."

"Sandy!" Jim Burnett's big voice boomed outside the door. "You in there, honey? I've got something to show you and Annette."

Annette ran to open the door. Mr. Burnett was standing there, holding a leather jewel case. He was wearing a broad smile on his ruddy face. Peggy Glaven was peeking past his shoulder, a warm smile on her lips.

"Come right in!" Annette said cordially, but her eyes couldn't help taking in the jewel case and she thought, Five thousand dollars! She's sold him something for five thousand dollars! Probably a string of pearls.

But it wasn't a string of pearls. When Sandy opened the leather case, she and Annette both caught their breath at the sight of a necklace of heavy antique gold set with glowing red stones.

"How lovely!" Annette exclaimed. "Rubies?"

"The very finest-quality, pigeon-blood rubies," Peggy Glaven told her. "My husband bought that necklace for me in Burma on our last trip to the Orient."

"It's terrific!" Sandy put down the case and held up the necklace so that the light would shine through the stones. Then she laid it back in the case and started to hand it to Mrs. Glaven.

Jim Burnett stopped her. "It's yours now, honey. Mrs. Glaven's been kind enough to let me buy it for you so you'll make a big hit at the hunt ball!"

"Oh, Dad! Really?" Sandy was thrilled. She hurried over to the dresser with the necklace held up around her neck to look at herself in the glass. "Oh, boy!"

But the clasp caught in the wool of her sweater, and when she tried hastily to loosen it, she dropped the necklace.

She scrambled for it and picked it up as her father shook his finger playfully at her and warned, "Be careful, honey. That cost your old dad five thousand big ones!"

"Wow!" Sandy's eyes were huge. "I'll certainly take care of it, Dad!" She looked at the necklace in awe.

"You'd better take out some insurance on it right away," Annette told Mr. Burnett laughingly. "It might disappear. I've always adored rubies, even though I never saw one up close before!"

Jim Burnett chuckled. "I'm not worrying about *you*, Annette. But I'm glad you mentioned insurance. I'll tend to that right away." He turned to Mrs. Glaven. "Who handles your policy on it now?"

She shook her head and lowered her eyes. "I'm afraid I haven't bothered with insurance since my husband passed away. He had it insured, and the policy ran out, and—oh, dear, I'm just not a good businesswoman!"

"Well, it doesn't matter. I'll run into San Benito tomorrow and find a good appraiser who deals with a reputable insurance company," Jim Burnett declared.

Mrs. Glaven pouted. "But we promised the Wilsons we'd drive up the coast to Rocky Point for a picnic tomorrow morning. We'll be gone all day."

"I'm sorry. I'd rather get this off my mind," he

told her good-naturedly. "I'll call Wilson and explain."

"Don't trouble," Mrs. Glaven said coldly. "I'll attend to it. But it seems ridiculous to me. Nothing has happened to that jewelry in all these years, and there's no reason to dash madly to insure it now."

"Just good business," Jim Burnett told her. "I don't want my little girl having to worry about losing the thing."

Mrs. Glaven turned abruptly and walked out. Annette saw her face. It was set and hard.

Now, why, Annette wondered, would she be that angry over a broken date?

11   *Missing: One Cap*

Annette and Sandy rode out along the trail toward the old adobe. Sandy had improved so much in her riding that she almost beat Annette in a little race along a smooth stretch.

"Next time I'll win, you wait and see!" She laughed breathlessly as they stopped to rest. "I'm almost looking forward to that fox hunt now!"

They had stopped in the shade of a sprawling oak tree, and almost the moment Sandy had stopped speaking, she gave a little shriek. A gray mockingbird had come swooping by, squawking impudently as it narrowly missed her head. High in the tree, a second one broke into a tuneful series of notes.

"Sassy things!" Annette laughed. "They must have a nest up there!" She tried to locate it among the branches.

"Come on!" Sandy urged. "Don't you want to talk to Brod?"

"Of course!" Annette agreed. "But there's lots of time. He'll be there all afternoon, probably."

"Oh, come on, Annette. Please?" Sandy begged.

"But I'm bird-watching," Annette teased. Then she relented. "Why don't you run on by yourself? I'll be along in a few minutes."

"Oh, okay! Come whenever you feel like it. S'long!" And before Annette could say anything more, Sandy had nudged her horse and was cantering off toward the branch trail that led up and over the hill to the adobe house.

Annette grinned and cocked an eye up at one of the mockingbirds. It was perched a few feet away, and still scolding her. "I know—I'm a third party here, too. But you've got to put up with me for a few minutes more and let the course of true love get off to a good start!"

And she slid out of her saddle and stretched out on her back under the tree. "Ten minutes should give them time to look into each other's eyes without somebody else standing around, gaping," she said, yawning.

But she had been there less time than that when the sudden pounding of hooves brought her out of a near doze. She sat up quickly to see Sandy riding toward her at a rapid trot.

She could see by Sandy's expression as her friend dismounted a few feet away that something had happened to upset her. "Wasn't he there?" she called.

Sandy threw herself down beside Annette before she answered. Her eyes flashed angrily. "Oh, yes, he was there, all right. And he can stay right there, by himself, as far as I'm concerned."

Annette raised an eyebrow. It sounded as if there had been a lovers' quarrel. It must have exploded suddenly, to say the least. She waited a moment for Sandy to go ahead, but Sandy just sat and sulked.

"Did you find out if he located that will among his father's papers?" Annette asked after an empty pause.

"He didn't," Sandy said flatly.

"Did he look through all the books for it?" Annette persisted.

"I didn't have time to ask him." Sandy's frown had melted, and she was rapidly getting to the tearful stage. "I mentioned that Dad had bought me Mrs. Glaven's ruby necklace, and he blew up! He shouted at me as if it were something terrible Dad had done."

"Why? Did he say why?" Annette asked.

"He said she had no right to peddle—that's just what he said—*peddle* his mother's jewelry! He said it was all his, and she was just trying to peddle it before he could find the will and prove he had a right to it!"

"Well, one of them isn't telling the truth! *She* said Mr. Glaven bought it in the Orient for *her*! Maybe it's another necklace, at that!"

Sandy shook her head. "No, I described it to him. And he said that was it, all right."

"Well, it's not your father's fault. All he did was put out good money for it."

"That's what I told him!" Sandy forgot her tears, in resentment. "And he said, 'Go ahead and wear it while you can. You may not have it very long!' And I told him he was mean and selfish and unfair, and I ran away."

Annette sighed. "It's too bad. I feel sorry for him."

"You do?" Sandy looked surprised.

Annette nodded soberly, and Sandy said meekly, "I guess I sort of lost *my* temper, too. Do you think I'd better go back and say I'm sorry?"

"Goodness, no! Give him time to cool down. He'll probably phone you tonight and apologize all over the place!"

"I hope you're right!" Sandy sighed. Annette noticed that she looked back in the direction of the adobe house as if she still felt tempted to return to it.

But she didn't say anymore about it, and they were soon mounted and riding homeward.

As they came in the front door, Mrs. Glaven was coming down the stairs toward them in more of a hurry than was usual for her. It was almost as if she had been waiting for them. Annette noticed that she was staring at Sandy's neck with a peculiar expression. I bet she thinks Sandy's been wearing that ruby necklace on horseback! she thought. Not that it's any of her business now that she's sold it.

"Did you have a pleasant ride, girls?" Mrs. Glaven asked, using her sweetest tones.

"Oh, yes, thanks," Annette answered politely. But Sandy just nodded and walked around her hostess and up the stairs.

Mrs. Glaven stared up after her a moment, became aware that Annette was, in turn, staring at *her*, and fluttered away toward the kitchen "to check on dinner."

When Annette entered Sandy's room a moment later, she found Sandy standing in front of her dresser, holding the leather jewel case. It was open and empty.

"This was shut when I left here," Sandy said angrily. "Somebody's been snooping!"

"Wh-where's the necklace? Did they take it?" Annette was alarmed.

"It wasn't here to take. I guess that's the only reason they didn't!" Sandy told her grimly. Then she crossed the room quickly and upended a small china vase that stood on the mantel over the fire-place. The necklace dropped out into her hand.

"You hid it," Annette said, relieved. "That was pretty smart of you. But why didn't you let Mrs. Glaven put it into her wall safe again till you want to wear it?"

"Because it's mine now, and if I want to wear it at breakfast or while swimming, I'm going to do it, even if it's vulgar!" Sandy said defiantly. "And I think I'll wear it to town this afternoon, right now, and let Mr. Brod Glaven see it!"

"You'll only get him all steamed up again," Annette argued. "I don't think it's very kind."

"I suppose not." Sandy was suddenly down-cast. Then she said thoughtfully, "I bet it was old Mary who opened that case. She's the only one who has the run of the upstairs, isn't she?"

Annette shook her head. "Nope. There's somebody else. Guess?"

"How can I?" Sandy replied.

"Sniff a little. What does it smell like in here?"

Sandy sniffed several times before she made up her mind. "Violets?"

"Right! Parma violets. The perfume of romance, tra-la! You've been surrounded by it for the last week or ten days," Annette said.

"Mrs. Glaven!" Sandy exclaimed. "But why would she want to steal back her necklace?"

"She wouldn't. Don't you see, she probably was worried about your leaving it out of the safe and came to see if it was out of sight."

"I don't think it's any of her business! And I don't like her snooping in my room," Sandy said stiffly.

"She was probably doing you a favor, or trying to," Annette insisted. "I think it was nice of her."

"All right, I guess it was, at that," Sandy conceded. "Well, she can stop worrying after tomorrow. Dad will have it covered by insurance."

"Fine," Annette said with a nod. "Then nobody will have to—" She broke off as she heard a famil- iar roar from the driveway. Sandy heard it at the same moment, and they both ran to the window.

"Brod!" Sandy started toward the door,

but Annette took hold of her arm hastily.

"Wait, Sandy," she advised. "He may not be coming to see you. Even from up here I can see the scowl. It looks to me as if he intends to have another row with Mrs. Glaven. Better stay out of it."

Sandy took another quick look at the young man who was out of the car and striding toward the front door. "He does look a bit upset. Maybe you're right."

So they waited where they were. And a few minutes later, when he went striding out of the house again and jumped into his car to speed away, they were glad they hadn't gotten mixed up in the family quarrel.

He disappeared down the driveway, his hair blowing wildly.

"Wonder where his red-and-white cap is today?" Annette grinned. "Seems funny to see him without it."

"I didn't see it out at the adobe before. Maybe he got tired of wearing it."

"Or he lost it last night when he came to say

good-bye to Black Prince!" Annette guessed excitedly. "I'm sure that's what happened."

"Was he wearing it then, do you remember?"

Annette nodded vigorously. "I'm sure of it. I noticed it on him when he was crossing the lawn toward the stable. That's one way I recognized him. And later, he didn't have it on. I remember distinctly that all the time he was talking calmly, he kept running his hand through his hair. He must have lost his cap in the scuffle with Higgins!"

"I wonder why nobody found it on the ground?" Sandy asked, puzzled.

"Maybe it didn't fall off till he ran into the stall to hide. It could still be there, because they probably wouldn't have any reason to go into that stall unless they needed it for a new horse," Annette said.

"I'm going to find it and hide it!" Sandy said excitedly.

But when she stole out of the house a little later, there was no sign of the red-and-white car cap. If it had ever been in the stall, someone else had found it first.

12 *Robbery*

"I think I'll call Brod at the gas station," Sandy told Annette casually, as they dressed to go down to dinner later that evening. "I'll ask him about the cap." She dabbed a last fluff of powder on her tip-tilted nose and added, "He'll want to apologize for shouting at me this afternoon—I guess." She wasn't too certain.

"He should," Annette mischievously assured her. "But don't get into another spat with him before you find out why he came here this afternoon. I'm dying to know."

"I'm sure it was the necklace," Sandy said soberly. "I wonder if I should offer to give it to Brod. I don't want to keep it if it's going to make him angry."

"Your dad wouldn't like that very much, Sandy," Annette told her seriously. "It would be like telling him it didn't mean a thing to you after he's been so pleased at being able to give it to you."

Sandy looked worried. "I guess it *would* hurt Dad's feelings. I wouldn't want to do that for anything."

Annette had a sudden thought. "Maybe he didn't come to see Mrs. Glaven about the necklace. Maybe he had a new idea as to where he could look for that will—someplace inside this house, most likely. And she wouldn't let him try," Annette suggested.

Sandy brightened. "But if he'd tell us, we could look for it there. Why don't I call him right away? This is his night at the station!"

Even before Annette could agree that it might be a good idea, Sandy was on the phone and ringing the gas station. But after a very short conversation with someone there, she set the receiver in its cradle and turned a disappointed face to Annette. "He's not there. The man says he called in to say that he was taking the night off for something important." She frowned. "I wonder if he has a big date with somebody."

Annette was tempted to tease her about being jealous, but she held back and suggested instead that Brod had probably driven out to the adobe to try once again to find the will among his father's papers. Sandy was eager to agree, once Annette had given her the idea, and they were soon on their way downstairs to the dining room.

They weren't left guessing very long about why Brod had come to see his stepmother. She was almost tearful as she told Sandy's father, "I don't know what I am going to do about that awful boy! He was dreadfully rude to me again today! He's found out somehow that I sold the necklace, and he demanded that I get it back from you at once and hand it over to him. When I refused and reminded him that I had every right to sell my own property, he made threats!"

"Seems to me it's time you talked to the police about him again!" Jim Burnett growled. "He's got to stop threatening you. That's breaking the peace, and you don't have to put up with it, no matter who he is!"

"He didn't threaten *me* alone," Mrs. Glaven

said, correcting Mr. Burnett. "He also promised to make trouble for you and the dear child here. He swore he'd get possession of that necklace even if he had to steal it! And I'm terribly afraid that he means it!"

"We'll soon find out!" Burnett was angry now. "When I take the necklace in to be appraised and insured tomorrow morning, I'm going to stop by police headquarters and talk to them about that boy. What he needs is a good long talking-to by the law!"

Sandy's eyes flashed angrily and her chin went up. Annette saw that she was about to speak up for Brod.

But that would let Mrs. Glaven know that they had met him and were on his side. So Annette caught Sandy's eye by spilling a glass of water and exclaiming, "Oh, I'm so sorry!"

And while Mrs. Glaven was ringing for the butler to come clear it away, Annette shook her head warningly at Sandy, and Sandy understood.

"Mrs. Glaven, I'm sorry I was so clumsy," Annette said. "I guess I got interested in what you folks were saying and just wasn't watching."

But Mrs. Glaven was quite gracious about it, and Annette felt certain that she hadn't guessed that the "accident" had been deliberate.

As soon as they could do it gracefully, the two girls excused themselves from the table and strolled outside to watch the sunset from a sheltered spot near the tall hedge.

Sandy was still angry about the things Mrs. Glaven had said about Brod. "Why didn't you let me tell her that he never, ever would have said such mean things?" she demanded crossly.

"Because we don't want her to know that we know Brod, or she'll watch us and we won't have a chance of helping to find that will."

"Golly, Annette, you think of everything! Thanks for stopping me! I'm a dope!" Sandy was contrite.

Annette laid a hand on Sandy's arm and nodded toward a tall young figure who had suddenly appeared from the direction of the stable.

"Brod!" Sandy started to get up and hurry to

meet him, but Annette stopped her. "Wait a minute. That's not Brod," she whispered. "Let's move back out of sight. It's Higgins, the stable man. I wonder what he's going to the house for—and right to the front door, too!"

They stepped to the rear of the hedge and watched as the young man swaggered up the lawn and stood staring at the front of the house for a minute or two.

"Maybe he's going to ask for a raise because he's got that new job guarding the stable every night," Annette whispered with a grin.

"Who told you that?" Sandy whispered back, puzzled.

"Mary, our fountain of information," Annette said with a giggle, and then suppressed it with her hand over her mouth.

"Well, if Dad buys this place, Higgins is one character who won't be with us. He's too surly and rude."

"I don't blame you," Annette agreed. "He snapped my head off this morning when I asked him to treat a brush scratch on Lucky's leg. Said he had more important things to do. So I did it myself."

The lights of a car were turning in down at the gate, and the young stable man hurried off, almost at a run, toward the stable. It seemed to them that he didn't wish to be seen.

"He knows he wasn't hired to guard the house, only the stable," Annette commented.

Sandy was looking very sober now. "Annette, I really think I should tell Dad about knowing Brod. I believe I'll ride into town with him in the morning when he takes my necklace to the insurance people."

Annette looked serious, too, as Sandy finished. "That's a good idea," she agreed. "When you tell him how harmless Brod is, and what it's all about, your dad won't go to the police station."

"That's exactly what I'm hoping," Sandy said quietly.

The big car had stopped in the driveway. A group of people got out and were admitted by Harmon, the butler.

Lights went on in the downstairs sitting room a few minutes later, and a couple of other cars full of guests arrived.

"What's going on?" Annette asked.

"The hunt committee is having a bridge party," Sandy said, sulking. "And Dad says he expects me to watch and learn how to play."

"It's not really painful once you get used to having your head chewed off every time you make a mistake," Annette assured her teasingly.

"I know I'll be bad at it," Sandy admitted. "And I would much rather learn how to put a racing car together. Brod's promised to teach me, you know."

"I'm sure that ought to make you a social success," Annette said with a laugh.

"SANDY! You're wanted in here!" It was Jim Burnett's oil-field bellow. He stood on the front step, peering around in the darkness for her.

"Yes, Dad! Coming!" she called back. "How about coming in and giving me some pointers?" she asked as they went in.

"Not me!" Annette teased as they stood at the

foot of the stairs. "I'm going to finish my letter to Aunt Lila. And no interruptions from people's boyfriends, I hope!"

"What was that?" Jim Burnett paused at the door of the sitting room. "What boyfriends?"

"Just a joke, Mr. Burnett," Annette assured him hastily.

Sandy wrinkled her nose at Annette. "Promise you'll come to my rescue as soon as you finish your letter?"

"Cross my heart!" Annette promised. "Go in and suffer alone a few minutes. I'll be with you as soon as I can."

Then she ran upstairs while Sandy went reluctantly with her father.

It was very peaceful in Annette's room, and she dashed her letter off quickly. She made no mention of the feud between her hostess and young Brod Glaven. It would take too much explaining right now. She decided to save it for later, when she was home again and having one of her comfortable long chats with Aunt Lila.

She added a postscript. "I think it's pretty

certain now," she wrote, "that the Burnetts will buy this estate. Mr. Burnett has bought a gorgeous horse named Black Prince, and Sandy's found a nice boy with the most fascinating mop of sandy hair—" She stopped writing as she heard light steps go by her door. A moment later, she heard Sandy's door open and close softly.

But Sandy was supposed to be waiting downstairs for her. And it wasn't like Sandy to go by so quietly and not at least pop her head in and say good night.

Something must have happened downstairs that Sandy didn't want to tell her about. The games were still going on, because the talking was as loud and boisterous as ever.

Almost at once, she decided she could guess what the trouble was. Sandy had exchanged words with Mrs. Glaven about Brod! Something had probably been said, and Sandy had lost her temper and defended him.

She sat thinking about it a few minutes. There wasn't much she could say to Sandy that would help. Sandy probably realized she had made a mistake the moment she had said whatever it was. But Annette felt that she ought to go in and offer a shoulder to cry on. It would help a little.

She went out into the hallway and over to Sandy's door. Better knock, she decided, and give her a chance to pull herself together before I go in. She's probably crying.

There was no answer to her first knock, so she knocked a second time, a bit harder. "Sandy," she called softly, "it's me. May I come in?"

For a brief moment there was no reply, but she could hear movement in the room. Then she heard a faint, muffled "come in."

It sounded as if Sandy was crying again, and Annette felt half sympathetic and half annoyed at her friend. She opened the door and started in. "I suppose there's no use asking what—" she began to say. But she had no time to finish. Something soft and smothering that felt like a woolen blanket came down over her head and shoulders and stifled her surprised shriek.

Annette struggled hard to free herself and call out for help, but someone was holding the blanket tight around her head, and every second it was getting harder and harder to breathe. She tried desperately to reach back and grasp her attacker, but her head was starting to swim and there was no strength in her arms. And then everything went black, and she felt herself falling.

13 *Clues*

There were excited voices around Annette when she regained consciousness. She found herself propped up on the floor, with Sandy's arm around her. A soft woolly blanket from Sandy's bed was still partly over her shoulders.

Jim Burnett and Mrs. Glaven were standing beside her, both of them looking shocked and worried, and the maid, Mary, was wringing her hands and sniffing back tears as she watched.

"Annette! Whatever happened? Are you all right now?" Sandy fired the questions at her the moment she saw Annette's eyes open.

"I—I guess so." Annette still felt a little faint.

"What happened?" Jim Burnett repeated his daughter's question anxiously.

Annette sat up, holding her head. "I thought I heard Sandy come in here, and I popped in to talk to her. But someone was waiting and threw this blanket over my head so I could hardly breathe. Then I guess I just fainted. That's all."

"Did you get a good look at him? Who was it?" Mrs. Glaven demanded sharply.

"He came from behind me. There was no chance of seeing who it was," Annette explained.

"There's nobody outside now, sir." Harmon the butler had come hurrying in. "But Higgins thinks he saw a man running off across the back lawn a couple of minutes ago."

Jim Burnett looked grim as he helped Annette into a chair. "I probably scared him off. We had said good night to the Wilsons at their car, and Mrs. Glaven and I were coming in when we heard someone run through the upper hall here. But when I got to the head of the stairs, he had already jumped out of the window to the back porch and was gone."

"So we looked and found you," Mrs. Glaven told Annette.

"But why would anybody—?" Sandy started to say, when Mrs. Glaven interrupted hastily.

"Oh, dear! The necklace! That's it! He came

to steal the necklace!" She was suddenly hysterical.

"Where is it, Sandy? Is it safe?" Mr. Burnett
demanded.

Sandy hurried to her dresser and picked up the
closed jewel case. "Here it is, Dad. Safe and
sound. I meant to hide it, but I forgot." She
brought it to him triumphantly. But when he
snapped it open, the necklace was gone.

"I knew it! I knew it! He said he'd do anything to get his hands on it!" Mrs. Glaven
exclaimed tearfully.

"Who did?" Sandy demanded with a scowl.
But she already knew what Mrs. Glaven's
answer would be.

"Brod, of course!" Mrs. Glaven snapped.

"We'd better notify the police right now!" Mr.
Burnett looked grim and determined.

"No!" Sandy's eyes flashed. "You have no
proof that Brod did this! It could have been anybody—maybe even one of your bridge players
could have sneaked up here!"

"Sandy!" Jim Burnett was shocked. "What do

you know about Brod Glaven? Where did you meet him?"

Sandy frowned and stuck out her chin. "Oh, around. And I know he wouldn't steal anything, neither a horse nor a ruby necklace, even though they both are his by rights!" She glared at Mrs. Glaven, and Mrs. Glaven glared back.

"That's enough, Sandy!" Her father's face was stern.

Annette spoke up quickly. "I know Brod, too, Mr. Burnett, and I'm sure he wasn't the man who was in here. I smelled tobacco smoke on whoever it was that tried to smother me. I've never seen Brod smoke."

"He doesn't!" Sandy agreed quickly. "He told me so!"

"Nonsense! The boy has smoked ever since he was in high school!" Brod's stepmother said angrily. "I'm afraid you girls have been fooled by my stepson in more ways than one. He's a spiteful, dangerous liar!"

"I don't believe it!" Sandy's eyes sparked fire.

"We're not getting anywhere, standing around

arguing. This is a case for the police and I'm going to call them right now!" Jim Burnett strode to the telephone. "We'll let them decide who did or didn't."

Old Mary bent quickly and picked up something that had been lying a few feet away from the blanket on the floor. She tried to hide it in the folds of her skirt without letting anyone see it, but Mrs. Glaven pounced on her and grabbed it from her hand. "Here! Give me that!"

It was a red-and-white cap.

Annette and Sandy exchanged horrified looks. They knew that cap only too well. And this was the last place they had expected to see it.

"There! I told you!" Mrs. Glaven waved the cap in Jim Burnett's face. "Look at the initials on the band! 'B.G.!' What more evidence do any of you need?" She turned to the girls as Jim Burnett took the cap and soberly examined it.

But the girls had no answer this time. All they could do was stand, looking unhappily at the cap, and wonder what the police would say.

They weren't left in doubt very long. Young

Sergeant Atwater came promptly. He was a blunt young man with a sharp eye and a small black notebook. When he had finished his investigation and talked one by one with the household staff and the guests, he snapped the notebook shut and told Jim Burnett, "We'll not jump to conclusions, sir, but I believe I'll go have a talk with young Mr. Glaven. There seem to be grounds for considering him a prime suspect."

"I could have told you that half an hour ago," Mrs. Glaven told him cuttingly. "It seems to me that the police waste a lot of time questioning the wrong people."

Sergeant Atwater's face reddened, but he continued to smile politely as he took his leave.

Jim Burnett walked out to the car with him, while Mrs. Glaven bade the girls a curt good night and went to her room.

The moment she was out of earshot, Sandy turned to Annette. "Oh, Annette! I still can't believe Brod took my necklace, no matter what anybody says."

"I don't believe it, either," Annette assured

her. "But just to be on the safe side, in case he did do such a silly, reckless thing, maybe we can get him to give it back if we get to him before the police do!"

"I'll go! Right now!" Sandy said, starting for the door.

"No wait! It's better for me to go. Your father will want to talk to you, I'm sure. And if he can't find you, he'll be very suspicious."

"Okay, then," Sandy agreed reluctantly. "But hurry!"

Sergeant Atwater was still beside the police car, talking to Jim Burnett, when Annette stole out the kitchen door and scurried to her car in the carport.

She climbed in and sat watching the police car, its red light blinking. When the sergeant pulled away a minute later, she waited only long enough for his car to drive out into the road to San Benito before she followed.

She was not sure just how she could get to Brod before the sergeant did, but she grimly followed the police car at a discreet distance. Then, to her relief, she saw him stop the car in front of a tall brick building with a sign on it reading SAN BENITO POLICE HEADQUARTERS.

Sergeant Atwater got out of the car and went briskly into the building. If he was getting a warrant for Brod, it would take him a little while to have it made out—time enough for her to get Brod's home address from the other attendant at the gas station.

The station was closed, and her heart sank. But the small card in the corner of the window had Brod's address on it.

She drove there swiftly and parked her car two houses beyond. Then she hurried toward his rooming house, wondering uneasily what she would say to the landlady. She had gone no farther than the gate when she saw the police car coming around the corner half a block away, with its red light blinking. It slowed down, its driver flashing a spotlight at the numbers of the houses as he approached.

There was nothing Annette could do. She walked back to her car and got in, just missing

the beam of the spotlight as it passed. As she drove away, she saw the police car stop at Brod's rooming house.

The Glaven house was dark as Annette put the Monster in the carport and went gloomily to the kitchen door. She had left it on the latch, but it was locked now.

She had a moment of panic before the door was unlocked, and Mary showed her anxious face.

"Oh, I'm sorry I got you up!" Annette said.

"Come in, darlin'," old Mary whispered. "You didn't get us up. We saw you go, an' we waited for you."

Old Patrick materialized in the darkness. "Did you see the poor lad and warn him the coppers were after him?" Patrick whispered.

"I didn't even get a chance to see him," Annette told them unhappily.

"Well, best be off to bed, miss. They won't be holding him long, if they *do* find him. It's all a mistake, you can count on it," Patrick assured her, and Mary agreed.

But a few minutes later in Sandy's room, the two girls were not so confident.

"I'm absolutely sure *she* put that cap on the floor so Mary or somebody else would find it!" Sandy insisted. Then she looked gloomy. "But how did she get hold of it in the first place?"

Annette snapped her fingers suddenly. "Wait! Higgins had that scrap with Brod over Black Prince. Brod must have lost his cap, and Higgins must have found it that night. And Higgins is the one who planted that cap to put suspicion on Brod! He's the robber!"

"Let's go tell Dad right now!" Sandy bounced up out of her chair and started to switch on the light.

"No, wait! That's just our *idea* so far. We don't have any proof to go on. Your dad would ask Higgins questions, and Higgins would skip out. And people would think Brod was still mixed up in it. Mrs. Glaven would say so, I know."

"Guess you're right. But what can we do?" Sandy puzzled, a frown wrinkling her forehead. "He may skip out, anyhow."

"Not right away. That would look too suspicious." Annette was thinking hard. "I imagine he'll keep the necklace in his room till it's safe to leave, then maybe have a fight with old Patrick or something and quit. I know that's how I would do it, if I had stolen it."

Sandy stared at her with sudden, excited understanding. "If we can find it there, we can prove he's the robber!"

Annette nodded. "The only thing we'll have to do is to pick a time when he'll be busy at the stable to search his room."

"We'll have to find out which room is his," Sandy said eagerly. "Mary can tell us."

"Let's see if they're still up!" Annette said and hurried toward the door.

Sandy was close on her heels as they stole downstairs again to knock on Mary and Patrick's door behind the kitchen. And when they told what they were planning to do in the morning, the elderly servants gladly offered to do all they could to help.

"I'll pile some extra duties on that Higgins in

the mornin'," old Patrick promised, "so's he won't be bumpin' into you sudden-like."

"And I'll let you know when Harmon an' Dave an' the other stable man are havin' breakfast," Mary added, beaming. "I'll cook them some extra pancakes like they're always askin' for. That'll keep them from goin' back upstairs and maybe catchin' sight of you goin' or comin'."

14   *Rubles Are Red*

Annette was wide-awake when Mary came tiptoe-ing into her room the next morning to tell her that everything was fine for her and Sandy to do a thorough search of Higgins's room over the garage.

"The others are eatin' their heads off down in the kitchen," Mary said with a chuckle. "They'll be chompin' there for a good ten minutes or more. So wake Miss Sandy and get yourselves over there quick."

Then she scurried downstairs again to refill the hungry men's plates.

Annette dressed hastily and dashed in to wake Sandy. But the late hours the night before had been too much for Sandy. Annette shook her, whispered urgently to her, shook her again, and pulled off the blankets. But it was no use. Sandy only groaned, turned over, and buried her face more deeply in the pillows.

Time was ticking by fast. In just a few minutes, the servants might finish breakfast and decide to go back to their quarters over the garage. It was hopeless to wake Sandy and try to get her ready in time.

"All right, stay here and sleep," Annette told Sandy's buried ears. "I'll go alone!" And she hurried away and out of the house as stealthily as she could.

It was only a short distance to the garage sleeping quarters, and Annette met no one on the way. No one was in sight over at the stables, either. She ran around to the rear of the building and up the outdoor stairway.

Mary had told her which was Higgins's room, and she hurried to it as quietly as the creaky stairs allowed.

The door was open, and she ventured in. The room was an untidy mess, clothing thrown on the floor, bed unmade.

There were few furnishings: a cot, a dresser, and a straight chair. A closet door stood open to reveal a collection of rather loud clothing. And

over everything, there hung the smell of rank
stale cigarette smoke.

She couldn't decide for a moment where to
start her search for the missing necklace. She
hated to touch any of the mess. Then, while she
was still hesitating, she heard a heavy-footed person come up the outside stairs, whistling a happy
little tune. Annette knew that tune. It was the
same one that she and Sandy had heard Higgins
whistling while they watched him studying the
front of the main house in the moonlight.

Now the steps were coming along the uncar-
peted hall.

Annette looked around desperately. There was
no hope of hiding under the narrow cot. He'd see
her the moment he opened the door. There was
only one place to hide—the small clothes closet.

She darted into the closet and cowered among
a collection of suits and coats that reeked of
tobacco smoke. There wasn't even time to close
the closet door fully before she heard the door to
the hall open and the whistler enter. She peered
out through the crack, shaking.

She expected that any second the closet door would be flung open, and she would be dragged out of hiding to explain what she had been doing there. But, to her immense relief, Higgins merely crossed the room to his dresser and, still whistling happily, unlocked the small top drawer.

His back was toward her, and she couldn't see what it was that he took out of the drawer. But she felt certain from the sound that the thing was wrapped in tissue paper. He stuffed it into his pocket and then slammed the drawer shut without bothering to lock it again.

He strode across the room, and a moment later Annette heard the door close and his footsteps clunk away.

Her knees were so weak that she had to lean against the wall for a couple of minutes before she could venture out of the closet. When she did come out, she tiptoed to the single window and stared down through the thin cotton curtain. She was just in time to see Higgins striding away.

But he was not going toward the stable. He

was going toward the service yard behind the kitchen wing.

Then she heard Patrick's voice. "Hey, you! What's the idea of leavin' your job half done, ye shiftless gossoon?"

Higgins stopped to glare back at him, started to retort, seemed to think better of it, and turned away again. As he swaggered off, he was whistling merrily as if to show his contempt for Patrick and his orders.

Annette waited only until Higgins had gone out of sight behind the kitchen wing, and then she hurried out of the room, sped downstairs, and followed him.

She was curious to see where he was going in such a hurry.

As she passed by the kitchen door, Dave the chauffeur came out, his cap on the back of his head and a toothpick stuck in one corner of his mouth.

At the sight of Annette, he hurriedly dropped the toothpick and straightened his cap. "Looking for me, are you, Miss Annette?" His pleasant face wore a smile.

"Not exactly, Dave, but now that you're here, please don't forget to pick up Miss Burnett's and my riding togs at the tailor's. Tomorrow's the hunt, and we haven't even broken in our boots yet!" Annette said lightly.

"I'll tend to that little errand first thing, miss." Dave touched the brim of his cap and strode toward the garage.

As Annette glanced after him, she saw him go up the rear stairway, two steps at a time.

Seems as if my guardian angel's right on the job this morning, she told herself as he disappeared through the doorway at the head of the stairs. If I'd stopped to look around after Higgins left, I'd have run smack-dab into Dave!

She hurried along the side of the house and looked around the corner toward the service yard.

Higgins, his back toward her, was standing over the incinerator. He had the firebox open, and the flames were leaping high. She saw him reach into his pocket and bring out the tissue-wrapped object. He glanced at it briefly, then tossed it into the firebox.

He stood watching it for a few seconds. Then he picked up a couple of pieces of firewood from the woodpile and added them to the fire.

It struck Annette that he wanted a good, hot fire going, a fire that would destroy whatever it was that he had put into the flames.

She heard Harmon, the butler, as he thanked Mary for the good breakfast, and she knew that she had better get out of sight before he noticed her watching Higgins.

She turned and fled along the side of the house, ducking safely inside the front door without meeting anyone.

Sandy was still sleeping peacefully when Annette went in. The pillow covered most of her head. Annette shook her. "Wake up, sleepyhead," she told Sandy, and pulled a length of blond hair that spilled out from under the pillow.

"Ow!" Sandy sat up abruptly, blinking. "Is it daylight?"

"Been and gone," Annette told her. And when Sandy was awake a little more, she told her about going to Higgins's room and nearly being seen.

Sandy was a little angry with herself for a moment for having missed the excitement, but she soon forgot it as Annette went on to tell about the mysterious package wrapped in tissue that Higgins had disposed of.

"Love letters, do you suppose?" Sandy asked romantically.

"Hardly." Annette shook her head and grinned. "It was something that took a lot more heat than anything made of paper." She had a sudden thought that made her brown eyes sparkle with interest. "Do you suppose he's lost his nerve and decided that he'd better get rid of the stolen necklace?"

"Either that," Sandy said quickly, "or he's pried the rubies out of it and is getting rid of the gold part!"

There was a tap on the door, and Annette ran to open it. Mary had brought a tray of breakfast up to the girls.

Annette cleared a place for it, and Mary set it down.

"Well?" Mary folded her arms. "Did you find out where the rascal's got it hid?"

"We're not sure yet," Annette confessed, and then she explained what had happened.

"We'll soon find out what he's been up to," Mary assured them. "I'll be emptying the waste-baskets in an hour or so, as is me job. And if there's rubies in them ashes, I'll find them, if I have to poke for the rest of the mornin' and sneeze me head off doin' it!"

But it wasn't that difficult. The girls hadn't even started to try on their new riding habits before Mary was back with several scorched and partly melted globs of something that looked like red glass.

"There we are, little ladies!" she announced with a triumphant flourish as she set the worth-less-looking objects on Sandy's bedside table. "Rubies!"

"They look more like a lot of melted glass than rubies!" Sandy stared at them disgustedly.

"Sure do!" Annette agreed glumly.

"Could be he's broke one of the madam's imported wineglasses. They're that shade,"

Mary guessed disappointedly. "Our trouble's for nothing, likely."

But after Mary had gone unhappily back to work, Annette still studied the stones—or whatever they were.

Sandy was trying on her new riding habit. The boots were pinching and she wasn't very happy. "I don't think I'll go on that ride tomorrow," she announced. "I'm sure I'll fall off my horse at the first jump, the way I feel in these boots."

"Y'know," Annette said thoughtfully, "I think I'll take these to some jeweler in San Benito and have him tell me what they are."

"Goodness! I wouldn't do that! He'd call the police to come and get you, if they turned out to be the real thing!"

"I'll just take a couple. And I'll stop along the road to pick up some rocks and things and make believe I'm an amateur rock hound, hoping I've found something worth a lot of money!"

The afternoon was still young when Annette got into her car and sped off to San Benito.

There was a little jewelry store on a side

street, a store whose window was full of all sorts of jewelry. Some of the pieces were new; some were antiques that looked sad and tarnished.

The jeweler smiled as Annette dumped out her handbag and sorted out the small chunks of quartz and pretty rocks. He paused to look at the globs of red very briefly and then tossed them aside.

"Are those red ones worth anything?" Annette asked hopefully, with an innocent stare. "I was hoping they were rubies or something."

"I'm afraid not," the elderly man told her. "I'd like to say your little collection is worth a fortune, but these are only ruby-colored glass."

Annette was disappointed. She started to pick up her small store of rocks and glass. "If they were really rubies," she asked, "how much could I sell them for? I mean, for instance, what would *you* give me for them?"

The jeweler looked at her with sudden sharp suspicion. Annette didn't notice. She was stowing the globs of glass in her handbag.

And when she did look up to see why he didn't answer, he assumed an affable smile as he said, "That would depend on the depth of color and the weight. Not all rubies are valuable."

"I mean, if the rubies were as big as these chunks of glass and just about this color, would they be worth a lot?"

"Quite a sum," he said slowly. "A pigeon-blood ruby is more valuable than a diamond the same size. Are you thinking of investing in some?" He made it sound light and teasing.

Annette laughed. "Heavens, no! I was just curious." And a few minutes later, she was driving off.

The jeweler studied her car as it left the curb and disappeared into the traffic. Then he went to the phone and dialed a number.

Annette would have been alarmed if she could have heard who it was that he asked for at that number.

It was someone she had met the previous night for the first time—Sergeant Atwater of the San Benito Police Department!

15 *The Guilty One*

Annette bought a newspaper on her way home. Just as she had expected, the robbery at the Glaven house was headline news. But, strangely enough, there was no report of Brod Glaven's arrest. The account merely said that several suspects were being sought.

Sandy met her at the garage as Annette put away the Monster.

"Mrs. Glaven is furious!" she reported. "The police are looking everywhere for Brod, but they can't find him. Dad says they're watching the bus station and the airport, but he's sure Brod slipped out last night." Then she remembered. "What about the rubies? Were they real?"

Annette shook her head soberly. "False alarm. They were plain old glass. I guess Mary was right—they're pieces of a broken wineglass."

They both looked gloomy as they went back

to the house to dress and go for their last practice ride before the next day's hunt.

"Go light on breakfast, darlings!" Mrs. Glaven greeted them merrily as they came downstairs together the next morning. "And do hurry! Patrick and Higgins have already left with the horses, and we're due at the club in half an hour for the start."

"We'll keep it to orange juice and a bun," Annette promised.

Jim Burnett was having a quick cup of coffee in the breakfast room when the girls came in. He looked handsome in his smart new habit, and his ruddy face broke into a smile when he saw them.

He slipped an arm around Sandy's waist. "Got some news for you, honey. We're committed to buying this place now. I'm signing the papers at Wilson's office tomorrow morning."

"Oh, Dad!" Sandy pouted unhappily. "I don't want to live here. Please!"

Her father looked unusually stern. "There's been enough shilly-shallying, Sandy. Sometimes you say you're willing to live here, then you suddenly change your mind again. This time we're sticking to it!" He strode off to wait outside for them at the car.

Mary pushed open the door to the kitchen and looked around the room. When she saw that the girls were alone, she entered hurriedly.

"Somebody brought a message for you in the night," she told Sandy mysteriously. She produced a folded sheet of paper which she slipped into Sandy's hand. "The lad's all right, miss, and he says to come to you-know-where as soon as you can!"

She darted back to the kitchen as Sandy hastily opened the folded paper and read the note written on it.

"Annette! Brod's found it! He's finally found it!" Unconsciously, Sandy raised her voice. "It was the very last entry in his father's diary!" She thrust the paper into Annette's hand. "Here! Read it!"

Annette scanned the note quickly and then exclaimed in amazement. "And the diary was tucked in his father's hunting boots all this time! How do you like that?"

Neither thought of glancing toward the open hall door as they excitedly studied the note again. And neither heard Peggy Glaven's light steps on the thick hall carpet as she hurried away from that door and went out to join Jim Burnett in the waiting car. Her face was grim beneath its set smile, and her eyes were granite hard.

A moment before the hunt set out from the clubhouse, Annette was startled to recognize Sergeant Atwater among the red-coated riders.

"Why not?" Sandy shrugged. "He can't be detecting all the time. He's probably one of the elite in his off time."

"I don't like it," Annette said worriedly. "Suppose he sees us cut out from the others and follows us to see where we're going? He may suspect that Brod's around here somewhere. Maybe he joined the hunt just to see if anybody drops out and acts suspiciously."

"What are we going to do?" Sandy asked nervously.

"Well, he can't watch everybody. So just one of us might be able to cut away when we get near

the trail to the adobe," Annette said. "Maybe
you'd better go, and I'll keep an eye on the sergeant. If he tries to follow you, I'll catch up with
him and fake some sort of an accident to keep
him from trailing you."

Soon the hunt was off to a brilliant start with
a clamor of hounds and the notes of a bugle. The
riders swept across woods and fields and up and
down hills and over fences in pursuit of one
small red fox which they never caught. It was
exciting.

Sandy rode close to Annette, and Annette
was proud of her pupil as Sandy took a low jump
like an old-timer.

But, on arrangement, they began to slow
down a bit after a while and let the rest of the
hunt get well ahead. Then, pretending that something was wrong with one of Sandy's stirrups,
they stopped. And after a momentary confer-
ence, Sandy cut away and disappeared up into
the small side trail they had followed for the first
time a couple of days ago.

Annette turned her mount to follow the hunt,

and as she did, she saw a solitary rider, back on the trail. He was sitting motionless, watching her.

When the rider saw that she had spotted him, he wheeled his horse and cut off into the brush in the same general direction that Sandy had taken. He was not wearing the red coat of the hunters, so it was not Sergeant Atwater. But his figure seemed familiar.

Suddenly, she knew who it was. Higgins! And if Higgins were heading for the same place Sandy was, he might get there first. There would be another fight in which Brod might get hurt— *probably* would!

She rode after Sandy as fast as she could go, paying no attention to the scratchy underbrush.

Most of the trail was rocky, and it slowed her down. From time to time she came to soft sand and saw the hoofprints of Sandy's mare and the broken twigs where girl and horse had crashed through the encroaching bushes.

Then, halfway to the old adobe, a cross trail cut in. After that, Annette noticed double horseshoe tracks, the bigger and heavier horse's prints almost crushing out those of Sandy's little mare. Higgins was behind Sandy now.

With growing alarm, Annette urged her horse on recklessly. There was an abrupt turn in the trail, and then Annette saw Sandy sitting, dazed, in the middle of the narrow path, holding her head. The mare was gone.

Annette dismounted and ran to her. "Sandy! Are you hurt?"

"I don't think so!" Sandy let Annette help her to her feet. "I was making good time, and then another horse came up right behind me. Before I could turn around to look, something struck my horse and she reared and dumped me!"

"Our friend Higgins!" Annette told her grimly. "I'm afraid he's headed for the adobe, too. He must have found out that Brod has been hiding there."

"He'll turn Brod over to the police! And they won't believe Brod is innocent of stealing that necklace. We've got to get out there and stop him somehow."

"Maybe, if we surprise Higgins, we can help Brod make Higgins confess," Annette agreed. "I'm more sure than ever that it was Higgins who stole it."

They rode double the rest of the way and soon were in sight of the old adobe house. Sure enough, one of the Glaven horses was tied at the rail. It was the big bay gelding that Higgins usually rode.

They stopped at the edge of the woods, and Sandy slid off first. She started toward the adobe, but hesitated as Annette dismounted and ran after her. "Be careful," Annette whispered, and caught her arm. "Let's not give Higgins any warning that we're around till we decide what to do."

Sandy nodded after a moment's hesitation, and they moved hastily but quietly toward the adobe. The big door was standing open a few inches.

They heard Higgins's snarling voice. "You'll hand over that diary right now, or I'll—"

"Why do *you* want my father's will? What can it possibly mean to you?" Brod's voice sounded puzzled. "And who told you I had found it?"

"It means a nice fat thousand smackers, sonny boy," Higgins said with a laugh. "And never mind who told me! Just hand it over and quit askin' questions!"

The sounds of a scuffle erupted from the other side of the heavy oak door.

"Come on! We've got to help Brod!" Sandy said, snatching up a chunk of rock.

"Hold it!" Sergeant Atwater's voice said sharply.

And when they turned in surprise, he spoke with a frown to Annette. "Stay right here and don't try anything, miss. Keep an eye on her, Miss Burnett! She's young Glaven's accomplice!" And before either of the astounded girls could speak, he had drawn his gun and was running toward the adobe.

"Accomplice!" Annette was stunned as she turned to Sandy.

"He's an idiot!" Sandy snapped. "And I'll tell him so! Come on, before he mixes things up even more!"

But they had only gone a few steps when Brod came staggering out of the adobe, dragging a limp Higgins by one arm. He met Sergeant Atwater at the doorstep. "Here's your robber! He'll tell you anything you want to know about that necklace!"

16 *All Clear Sailing*

It was a little bewildering for a few moments, but Sergeant Atwater soon realized that he had been on the wrong track. He had been sure that Annette was involved in the theft of the ruby necklace and had faked the attack and robbery. The jeweler's report of her interest in the price of rubies had made him suspect her.

Now, suddenly, it seemed that neither Annette nor Brod was guilty. Higgins was not only willing to confess, through bruised lips, that he had taken the necklace but he was eager to put the blame on the one who had hired him to do it— Mrs. Glaven!

His confession, given later at Police Headquarters, explained why Mrs. Glaven had hired him to steal back and destroy the necklace. She had been desperate for money when she had sold her necklace to Jim Burnett. She had been almost certain that Burnett would finally decide to buy the estate for a good round sum. And when that happened, she would persuade him to sell back her necklace "for sentimental reasons" before he could find out that the rubies in it were only imitations. She had long since sold the real ones secretly, to pay the expenses of keeping up the estate so it could be sold.

Annette's suggestion that Mr. Burnett have the necklace insured at once had spoiled her plan. Only its theft could save her from exposure.

So she had hired Higgins to steal it and leave the car cap as evidence against young Brod. Her little plot had worked so well that she had gone a step further. She had heard enough that morning to know that Brod had found his father's handwritten will. She had sent Higgins to follow the girls to her stepson's hiding place and to get there first and obtain the will. Once it was in her hands, she had intended to destroy it, so she would not have to share the estate with Brod if the will called for it.

Confronted with Higgins's confession, Peggy Glaven tried to deny it all. But the evidence was too strong against her, and she was held for trial.

"I still feel sorry for her," Annette said soberly, as she and Sandy read the morning newspaper account of it the next day.

"So do I—I guess," Sandy admitted. "And so does Dad. He says he'll drop the fraud charge and just keep back five thousand out of the money he'll be paying for her half of the estate."

"Then you *are* buying it! It's settled at last!" Annette teased her laughingly. "Sure you won't change your mind again?"

Sandy shook her head and blushed. "No more. I'm afraid it's made up for good now."

Annette's dark eyes twinkled. "Unless Brod decides not to sell his half."

"Oh, but he's already agreed to let us buy it. And he's going to live in the adobe and fix up a garage out there for us to work on a racing car and—" She stopped abruptly and threw her arms around Annette in a real Burnett bear hug. "I'm so happy!"

"And I'm so glad!" Annette told her, returning the hug. "But Aunt Lila is neither happy nor glad!" She held up a letter that had just arrived. "She has a house full of guests and nobody to help her. So I'd better be leaving for home just as soon as I get packed!"

And in spite of Sandy's coaxing, that's just what Annette did.

The last glimpse that she had of Sandy that afternoon was a very different one from the first she had had at the airport, not so long ago. There was no makeup on Sandy's pert face now, only a smudge of grease. Instead of trailing a mink scarf, she was encased in an oversize pair of Brod's overalls and waving farewell with a wrench.

Annette was pleased about it all as she sped along the wide seashore drive that skirted the blue Pacific. She would have a story with a happy ending for Aunt Lila when she told her about the mystery at Moonstone Bay.